· LOVE IN VAIN ·

FEDERIGO TOZZI
Courtesy of the Mondadori Archive

LOVE IN VAIN

SELECTED STORIES OF
FEDERIGO TOZZI

■ ■ ■

TRANSLATED, WITH AN INTRODUCTION, BY
MINNA PROCTOR

A NEW DIRECTIONS BOOK

The stories in this collection were selected from *Tozzi, Le Novelle*, vols. 1 and 2, Vallecchi
Editore, Florence, 1988, and *Tozzi, Opere*, Arnoldo Mondadori Editore, Milan, 1987.

The following translations were originally published in *Conjunctions: 31* (1998): "L'Amore,"
"The Idiot," and "House for Sale." "The Clocks" first appeared in *The Republic of Letters*, "The
Tavern" in *Chicago Review*, "To Dream of Death" in *The Literary Review*.

**The translator would like to acknowledge her debts: for the assistance and contributions
provided by the Translation Committee of PEN American Center and the MacDowell
Colony; for invaluable support and editorial input, Madga Bogin and Peter Glassgold;
for all of the above and more, Benjamin Anastas, Allegra Bicocchi, Monica Sarsini,
and Arlene Zallman.**

Book design by Sylvia Frezzolini Severance
Manufactured in the United States of America
New Directions Books are published on acid-free paper.

First published as New Directions Paperbook 921 in 2001
Published simultaneously in Canada by Penguin Books Canada Limited

Library of Congress Cataloging-in-Publication Data

Tozzi, Federigo, 1883–1920.
  [Short stories. English. Selections]
  Love in vain: selected stories of Federigo Tozzi / translated,
with an introduction by Minna Proctor.
    p. cm.
  ISBN: 0-8112-1471-0 (pbk. : alk. paper)
    1. Tozzi, Federigo, 1883–1920—Translations into English.
  I. Proctor, Minna. II. Title.

PQ4843.O8 A27 2001
853'.912—dc21   00-052719

New Directions Books are published for James Laughlin
by New Directions Publishing Corporation,
80 Eighth Avenue, New York, NY 10011

CONTENTS

Tutto é stato per me
un passare tra la vita per
giungere a completare
la mia anima.

        —Novale

For me it has all been
a passing through life
in order to arrive at the
completion of my soul.

        —Novale

FEDERIGO TOZZI
(1883–1920)

On the eighth of November 1902, the following listing appeared on the back page of *La Tribuna*, a Siena newspaper: YOUNG LADY DESIRES EPISTOLARY CORRESPONDENCE. SEND INQUIRIES TO ANNALENA, POST SIENA.

Three friends answered the ad, one of them Federigo Tozzi, nineteen years old, who read the listing while at the barber shop, perhaps having his hair done "like Chopin," the look of choice among the young bohemian café set. "Annalena" was not taken with Federigo's first letter, which apparently stated he was pursuing the correspondence only in order to "study the character of a *young lady*." It was a crude appeal, for which he apologized in his second letter: "I shouldn't be writing again, considering that you never responded to my first letter . . . But I can't resist the ardent desire to communicate this way with a woman I don't know—so taken am I perhaps by the novelty of it." The second letter won him a response (though it didn't place him first among the applicants, a privilege that was still several exchanges away), and thus began the long correspondence between the writer Federigo Tozzi and Emma Palagi (aka Annalena) the woman who would become his wife, secretary, collaborator, and muse.

"At this moment," explained Federigo in an early letter, "I'm writing to you as best as I can because (and I want you to know this) I am in a . . . café and all around me there are people drinking, yelling, swearing, spitting . . . A friend interrupts me and wants to know what I'm doing, I punch him and put him in his place so I can keep on writing. This quick sketch will give you an idea of how I do things and let you know a bit of my life and the kind of company I keep. But don't think I'm *frivolous!* The external is rough, but deep inside me, touched only by harmony, I hold intact the purity of my spirit . . ." He signed the letter "Rudolfo," as he did all of them at the beginning. Young Federigo was at a crossroads. After a failed attempt at art school in Florence, Tozzi was in his native Siena, living in a hotel room at his father's expense. His relationship with Federigo Sr., a small landowner and successful restaurateur, was marked by frequent and violent conflicts over women and Federigo Jr.'s lack of direction. Upon his return from Florence, Tozzi finally renounced formal education, putting an end to a disastrous academic career. He had spent his childhood being expelled from one school after another due to *cattivo comportamento* (bad behavior). As a last resort, his mother had sent Federigo to a Franciscan monk for tutoring when he was twelve years old, a solution which promised success, but came to an abrupt end when his mother died later that same year. His father—ever contentious—had refused to pay the extra money for private lessons.

In 1902, Federigo was an active member of the local Socialist Party and spent his mornings reading "foreign authors" (Huysmans, Shakespeare, Schlegel, Hugo, Maupassant, Poe, Marx, Engels, Tolstoy, Darwin, Zola) and his evenings in cafés with like-minded gadabouts. His corre spondence with Annalena became compulsive (those letters now represent the richest biographical source on Tozzi's self-education). He wrote to her about what he was reading, his ideas about art and politics, and his love affair with a young woman he called Mimi, a pseudonym he'd chosen to compliment his own "*bohèmien*" handle, Rodolfo. It wasn't until that relationship fell apart in the spring of 1903 that Rodolfo and Annalena began writing to each other as Federigo and Emma, and though they still hadn't met, began adopting the intimate *tu* form of address.

Mimi's real name was Isola, and she was Federigo's first true love—theirs was a tale of temptation, class conflict, and betrayal, which later became the basis for Tozzi's first major novel, *Con gli occhi chiusi* ("With His Eyes Shut"). That the tale, drafted in 1913 and published in 1917, finds its first written form in his letters is typical of Tozzi, an author who plundered his own life for stories. His culture, environment, and circumstances recur throughout the work—farms in the hills of Siena, lascivious peasant women, drunken and abusive fathers, helpless, sickly mothers, and lovers who are idealized and inadequate at once. But it's Tozzi's fidelity to the emotional life of these worldly configurations, to a subtle and unsentimental truth-telling, that repeatedly transports his unassuming stories above and beyond provincial autobiography. According to Tozzi, the writer's gift and burden is to be an observer, one who doesn't shrink from the brutality of nature and ugliness of man, but who recognizes beauty in a gust of wind and God in a crippled goat.

Tozzi had been writing to Emma for five months when he discovered that his Isola was living in a brothel, pregnant by another man. "Isola no longer belongs to me," he revealed in a histrionic letter of 7 April 1903, "she belongs to everyone! . . . What has the sacrifice of my honor cost her?" At that moment, there was no more pristine affinity than the one Federigo felt for Emma—the bodiless and unsullied voice of reason and comfort to whom he'd confided everything, the woman who was irrefutably his intellectual match. Emma had been studying to become a nurse when her own mother died, and as the eldest daughter of a large family, she had been forced to quit her education and come home to Siena. Emma had placed the ad in *La Tribuna* hoping to find intelligent company. Tozzi satisfied that wish and more. From the very first, he wrote to her without censure: "When I think about writing you, I never concern myself with locating the intonation of the last letter. It is not I but my passions that command, the passions I let flow like a rain-soaked shepherd watches the water run. So I write according to whatever mood I find myself in, sad or happy, sweet or bitter, hateful or loving. Deep down, understand, I'm still the same: only the outer reaches of my conscience are mutable, because that is what comes into direct contact with external impressions— naturally my 'I' doesn't change." (13 December 1902) Federigo revealed to Emma his artistic ambitions (that he'd already written poems and stories in secret), defended and redefended his political beliefs, and argued with her passionately about religion (he was a staunch atheist then). At times, he wrote her with such brutal honesty that it would seem she was his alter ego: "Understand how you were the origin of this kind of spirituality. Understand how you gave birth to the discipline of this ambition. And as with extreme deprivation, I always clung to some fraction of your energy. Your fatal mistake was not writing me according to my new ambitions. Will it hurt if I tell you that last night I felt like crying?

But I wanted you to make me strong. I wouldn't love you if you didn't feel *equal* to me. And you are . . . " (15 September 1907). Later, Tozzi would refer to the stories he wrote and that she transcribed and edited as their children, such was the intensity of their artistic communion.

Yet Federigo and Emma were more perfect epistolary lovers than they ever were married lovers. Soon after their meeting in 1903, they separated for the first of many times, while Federigo pursued the decadent lifestyle he associated with being an "artist." The philandering was cut short in 1905, when Federigo suffered an illness that threatened his eyesight and kept him bedridden for several months. The biographical accounts vary—it might have been a venereal disease—and there is speculation that Emma nursed him during this time. Our primary source of biographical information about Tozzi from this period, however, is Emma herself, and in defense of her own dignity, she elected to remain vague about the circumstances of his illness. No matter what the specifics, Tozzi's brush with blindness seemed to bring him to a reckoning, and as soon as he recovered, he threw himself into his studies, distancing himself vituperatively from the company and lazy pastimes of his "former life." He found God and devoted himself to his education simultaneously. And he committed himself to Emma; in 1906 they were engaged. During the next two years, while Emma was in Rome working as a nurse, she became involved with a group of "educated women"—an association that inspired venomous jealousy in Federigo. "You're vile!" he wrote Emma after reading an essay she'd written about women and health care for a feminist journal. "Did you *have* to write that article?" He attempted to join her in Rome, but failed to find work there as a writer and returned to Siena in order to apply for a civic position at the post office or railroad.

Neither of the fathers would let Emma and Federigo marry until Federigo had secured an independent livelihood.

In the years following his illness, Tozzi read obsessively in the local library, determined to finish his education by playing the part of both teacher and student. It was a short but intense apprenticeship which followed no canonical rules, but rather the organic mayhem of literary genealogy: "What a muddle!" he wrote to Emma in June 1907.

> More poetics! From Dante to the Bible, from the Bible to Homer, from Homer to Plato, from Plato to Maeterlinck, from Maeterlinck to Leibniz, and from Leibniz to Dante, and so forth—a whirl of images. I'm embarrassed to even write it. My face has gone red. But how can I enforce any order if I have an appetite for all of them? In this very moment, Virgil's come to mind. . . .

Upon discovering Shakespeare—and *Hamlet* in particular—Tozzi didn't leave the house for five days straight. This kind of behavior, he reported to Emma, made people think he was crazy; his neighbors called him *il pazzo*. Lunacy was a particularly "romantic" notion in the early days of psychology, frequently associated with the artistic temperament, and Emma dutifully repeated the diagnosis in the biographical notes she wrote on her husband after his death. Tozzi was a consummate artist, devoted to his work and to literature at large; he was irritable and sensitive, morose at times; he clung to idealized notions; he suffered but never curbed his vices; he believed in true love and eventually in a Christian God; he was anything but crazy, although being so aware of the extremes of the human mind, and subject to the vertigo of intellectual endeavor, might have made a man think (or wish) he was going crazy:

Intellectually, I was highly variable. One day I was inundated by Christian mysticism, another day it would be the pagan imagination to transport my spirit. But it was all purely a game of the intellect. An investigation unto itself. I wanted to experience all kinds of moral interaction. People were sensations . . . . Even people's mannerisms became in my mind the object of intellectual spirituality. I didn't feel them. I analyzed them with my spirit, and believed I had possession of them. Men became creatures, like animals. I didn't see them as anything but hunks of meat with filthy intestines. I loved things and mostly I loved plants. In them I found my equal. And often I wished I could become a cornstalk.

Tozzi's work is remarkably faithful to the vacillations of the spirit exemplified in the passage above, to the mind's ability to empathize with, even adopt, contradictory beliefs and emotions. This kind of investigation is especially clear in the earlier stories included in this collection, which are more explicitly about the split between thought and action than the later work. In 1902, Tozzi wrote to Emma, "First love is so sweet! We ignore the woman but love her in order to experience love." Six years later, Tozzi turned the observation into "First Love," the story of an awkward adolescent courtship. The young couple has barely anything to say to each other, but dutifully perform the ritual:

Then Emilia smiled sweetly.
Why is she laughing? he thought. *Am I so ridiculous?*
And he attempted in vain to appear indifferent.
"We haven't ever kissed," she said suddenly.
Kiss you? But your lips scare me. And I'm not attracted to

them. I'll not give you any kisses. Nevertheless, he moved closer to her face and kissed her out of curiosity.

Tozzi's curiosity, his hunger to experience and understand life, meant he was in continuous and furious evolution, an evolution reflected in his fiction. He suffered every conflict as if it were his first, celebrated every civil conversation as if it were the dawn of happiness. The turbulence of his relationship with his father was a constant. Though his mother died when he was only thirteen, he tirelessly depicted and reinvented the maternal figure in his work, women who were fearful and reticent, women who loved imperfectly—"I've learned to live with my soul, now I must learn to live with my mother!"

The lovers in his stories are similarly volatile, clumsy, unreliable, unfaithful, and yet they pine for exaltation, ready to lose their souls in the heart of another. Tozzi the man, like Tozzi's fictional characters, was perennially capable of rebirth, of innocence, of hope—manifest themes that the writer was flirting with as early as 1906, during Emma and Federigo's second major round of correspondence.

> I force myself to reciprocate everything that I dream in you. And the events of my past are like a nightmare. You know how much I expect of you. I don't love you out of habit. I never want to be without a reason to love you. And I ask of you, forever, my resurrection . . .
>
> In you I've found that purity and beauty that I imagined so often while I was studying. And all of my thoughts are like a crown of flames.
>
> Yes, you are the eternal one that I've imagined. I've found in you what I've believed to be most pure, and I want you to lift me up always higher . . .

Oh, Emma! Understand that even my most awful jealousy comes out of how much I adore you. Because I know what evil is inside of me and all I need is your affirmation to be rid of it. But you must give me this affirmation. (13 June 1907)

The death of his father came unexpectedly in 1908, a mere two months after Federigo had finally secured a job on the rails in Florence, and before father and son had the chance to reconcile their differences. Federigo was devastated, but the inheritance enabled his marriage to Emma. He sold his father's successful restaurant, and the newlyweds moved to the family farm on the outskirts of Siena. Federigo didn't have a head for business and drove the farm to ruin in short order. But his ideology and literary endeavors during this time flourished. He worked with a series of magazines, including a publication he founded with his lifelong friend, the poet Domenico Giuliotti, called *La Torre*, billed as the "journal of the Italian spiritual response." And he met Giuseppe Antonio Borgese, the critic who would come to be Tozzi's most important literary patron, introducing him to the editors at Treves, the prestigious publishing house which six years later would start publishing his work. Emma gave birth to their first and only son, Glauco, in 1909. His first poems and stories began appearing in print in 1910. His amorous life also flourished during this time; he had no fewer than four lovers among the Sienese intelligentsia, passions which Federigo seemed ashamed of and kept secret even from Giuliotti, his other major correspondent. Predictably, these indiscretions and his failing finances put a strain on his marriage, though he wrote constantly through the upheaval and, according to Emma, the "manuscripts mounted." Still, his literary efforts weren't lucrative enough. In Emma's biographical notes, she describes these years as "the most unhappy and bitter for Federigo, because he was a player who'd gambled everything confident of victory—yet victory took delight in eluding him."

In 1914, Federigo followed one of his lovers to Rome. Emma and Glauco joined him later that year, but the couple soon separated again—their correspondence, however, continued unabated, focusing more intensely than ever on the subject of his writing. After failing again to find work as a writer, he volunteered for the Red Cross and went to work in its press office. There is a story written during this time and set in Rome called "The Lovers," a painfully realistic staging of a man and a woman trying to recover their damaged relationship:

> . . . he grabbed her shoulders and forced her to stand there and hug him. She grew even more resolute and pulled her face away. Then he let her go. He was too angry, and yet he agreed with her. She was better than he was. So he waited, his head lowered, for her to say a kind word. He was sorry that he hadn't loved her. But since he was sorry, and she must realize that, he didn't understand why she couldn't forgive him. She must be able to forgive him.

It is easy to imagine just this scene between Emma and Federigo, who were reconciled in 1916. For better or for worse, Emma was his muse, and their reconciliation marks the beginning of Federigo's most inspired and successful literary period. His first major publication, a book-length prose poem called *Bestie,* came out in 1917, followed by his big critical success, *Con gli occhi chiusi,* in 1919. He met the great

Sicilian writer Luigi Pirandello, who admired his work—likely recognizing the influence of fellow Sicilian Giovanni Verga. Pirandello was then working as an editor for the newspaper *Il Messaggero*, which published many of Tozzi's short stories and essays between the years 1918 and 1920. Tozzi's work was well received; he quit the Red Cross and was at long last able to live the literary life he'd aspired to for almost fifteen years. His second novel, *Tre croci* ("Three Crosses"), was published in early 1920, four days before Federigo fell mortally ill with the Spanish flu. He died suddenly on the 20th of March, and the novel's critical reception was overshadowed by the obituaries.

In just twelve years, Tozzi wrote 120 short stories, five novels, and two books of poetry, as well as plays, many essays, and piles of drafts, notes, and letters. In death as in life, Emma's love for her husband was made manifest in her commitment to his writing. In collaboration with Borgese, Emma oversaw the posthumous publication of a short story collection, his essays, three novels (one unfinished), and, eventually, the eight volumes of his complete works. Her efforts were temporarily quelled in 1925 after she was advised that the posthumous work was being interpreted an exploitation of Tozzi's marginalia and "lesser" achievements. Her final gesture, an attempt to explain the man behind the art, was the publication of the letters he wrote to her in *Novale*, a remarkable document of the young artist's formation, a testament to his devotion to truth and his profoundly spiritual capacity for love.

The title, an evocative but meaningless neologism, was suggested to Emma by none other than Luigi Pirandello. The first edition of *Novale* bore the subtitle "A Novel" on its jacket cover, the subtitle "A Diary" on its title page, and is described by Emma Tozzi in her introduction as "an autobiography." *Novale* is made up of Tozzi's letters to Emma, edited with such dramatic sensitivity that it could also be described as an epistolary romance—and a potboiler at that. Later editions, including a version reedited and annotated by Glauco Tozzi, eschew subtitles altogether, letting the book and its nonsensical title stand alone in the category of "literature." All of the subtitles are to some degree correct, as is no subtitle at all. This vexing situation—a stunning work of art culled from life that defies definition—is in a way the best paradigm with which to represent Tozzi's genius.

In the midst of a cultural revolution, innovation is difficult to contextualize, and even more difficult to accept. In his own time, Federigo Tozzi was generally misunderstood, ignored, or adopted as a mission by a select few evangelical literati. There is, however, no dearth of language to describe Tozzi's fiction, the best of it by his own hand. Ensconced in a minimalist but meticulous physical world, Tozzi was beholden to the facts of behavior and emotions, to the simple rendering of the strange and paradoxical passions of simple life, to what he termed "the mysterious acts of man." A great writer, according to Tozzi, was not a master of intricate or fabulous plot, but rather the writer who paused along the road to observe a man pick up a pebble and then let it drop back to the ground, only in order to continue on his way. "Everything consists in how humanity and nature are seen. The rest is secondary, even mediocre, and ugly."

Tozzi was a self-styled expert on "primitive" Sienese writers, spiritual texts like the letters of Saint Catherine of Siena (which he eventually edited and collected into a book called *Le cose più belle di Santa Caterina da Siena* published by the futurist celebrity Giovanni Papini) and her visionary counterpart Saint Teresa of Avila. He read Saint Bernardino of Siena and found in his journals a model of naturalistic writing:

> This prose style, limpid and lively, is based entirely on the sound of the voice—it follows no other rules. It breathes to this day, as if we were hearing it rather than reading it. There isn't a single sentence that doesn't bear the same tenderness, the same soaring of the soul that gave birth to it. It is prose full of sonorous sensations, which registers inside us like blessed memories. . . . *We modern writers should study it, we, who through our expression and in our style seek liberation from our sensations and states of mind.* He has the ability to teach us how to write without veils and the imposition of literary artifice, he gives us the idea that it is possible to bring to life even that which seems less susceptible to the written word. There is a world in us that seems destined to silence, and yet that world is perhaps the best of us and the most meaningful.

The investigation of naturalism, of truth, defined Tozzi's poetics. This was a literary moment of high style, of romanticism, early modernism, formalism—the art of verisimilitude was being subjected to new conventions. Impassioned by literature, yet isolated from the mainstream, Tozzi found nothing so fascinating as the unfettered expression of the inner lives of normal people. And that came as much from what he was reading as from the profound stimulation he found in his own life.

Any reader will recognize that Tozzi's work is not simply realistic. The lustful murder depicted in "Assunta," one of Tozzi's earliest short stories, is less plausible as true crime than it is as a revenge fantasy, an accurate representation of jealousy. This was the scope of realism that Tozzi sought. As he became a more skilled writer, his explorations of perception grew more subtle. His characters embrace as much illusion, or delusion, as is necessary for their peace of mind. In "To Dream of Death," an elderly woman who interprets her dreams as a hobby stages the circumstances of her own death — mitigating her fear of death by controlling it. Again, this story, by not questioning the superstitions of a character, truthfully engages the feeling of fear.

As in life, truth is difficult to embrace, difficult to comprehend. Moments of epiphany are muddled, often logically illegible. In "The Boardinghouse," an exacting love-hate story, Marta is a bitter widow incapable of understanding the complexity of her feelings toward her dying neighbor Gertrude:

> She could see so many roofs from where she sat high above them; they all seemed suspended in midair. The swallows hid under the drainpipes and built nests there. A peach tree in full bloom rose above the carefully cultivated green cypress gardens. The spring air didn't stir any memories, but it made her feel better, and she derived great pleasure from knowing that Gertrude was sick and couldn't see everything that she could see. Marta understood now, without understanding why, that she needed to live. She would open her window and lean out over the sill; she'd hold a bowl of scalding milk in her hands and dunk bread into it, while watching all that serenity spread out before her. She chewed slowly so she wouldn't finish her breakfast too quickly.

Tozzi's epiphanies are frustrated resolution. They arrive with all the illumination of a chain link fence dropped from the sky in the midst of a tornado. In "L'Amore," a man's passion for a married woman is thwarted by her clever husband. Through the dazzling use of reverse psychology, the husband leads the would-be lover into a state of inertia: "I turned toward Virginia, anxiety drowning my soul. She passed by the window, supple and tall, with long legs, and breasts like those of the most sublime Grecian statue. I realized that the moment had arrived in which I must speak; yet I was terrified by voluptuous anticipation. I fell to my knees."

Characters have epiphanies or transformations, but they aren't transformed themselves. Reality shifts, but that's because the characters are operating on reality through their perceptions. Reality itself becomes the subject rather than the *means*. In "The Crucifix," the narrator finds beauty in a young prostitute's misfortune, transforming the brutal circumstances of her life into a vision of divine martyrdom: ". . .by the church wall, the heat burns over the wooden crucifix, as if wanting to pull the nails from His feet and wrists. And the young girl awakens, as if rising from that pile of waste." The girl is "saved" only in the narrator's mind. "The Crucifix" opens *not* on the "banks of the Tiber" but in the imagination of the narrator, who sees before him a primordial "half-formed" world, a world in which Adam has yet to gain eyesight, in which Adam mistakes the wind on his skin for his own movement. "The imagination is like Adam's dream—he awoke and found it truth," wrote the poet John Keats (1795–1821) in a letter. "I am certain of nothing but the holiness of the heart's affections and the truth of the imagination." Keats represented a romantic movement that influenced Tozzi and also stood for an aesthetic of irrelevance he wanted to leave behind.

Tozzi read, studied, and participated in a turn-of-the-century society that was wrestling with the retrieval of belief and meaning from the crisis of the Enlightenment. Unlike the atheist formalists who built modernism out of scientific structures, Tozzi applied Catholic spirituality to his literature, forging a distinct realism that was based on psychology, insight, expressionism, and the truth of subjectivity. In his aphoristic novella *Barche Capovolte* ("Overturned Boats"), Tozzi wrote, "By now, we should recognize that the conscience is not an active force. It's an effect. And even if it at times resembles a gigantic eye, it doesn't substitute for the function of seeing."

The inept delusions of the retarded adult who narrates the story "The Idiot" reveal themselves as a terribly real testimony to the fact that the narrator's mind is too limited to escape through delusion. He can't even imagine a better life for himself. In "The Miracle," an unhappy librarian finds real solace in regression. He is delivered into the delusion that he is a child—because the illusion is more beautiful than the real. Yet Tozzi's fugue at once embraces the totality of unforgiving, often cruel reality.

Tozzi's era saw the explosion of popular psychology—the golden period before psychological archetypes began to replace character development in fiction. Italo Svevo (1861–1928) was at work on *The Confessions of Zeno*, his epic character study of a cigarette smoker in analysis. Pirandello was constructing grand surreal metaphors out of identity crises in *Six Characters in Search of an Author.* Tozzi consumed books of psychology: William James, Pierre Janet on hysteria and neuroses, and Théodule Ribot on adolescence. He was intrigued not by the *whys* of human behavior, but rather by the *whats* or the *hows.* Tozzi's stories assume that the mind is a vexing organ, subject to mysterious and yet terribly powerful impulses. Among the stories collected here, the theme of semiconscious and often self-defeating behavior recurs. In "Poverty," a debt-ridden farmer strikes out at his wife rather than admit he's failed her. In "Vile Creatures," a group of young prostitutes inspire sympathy in a client by simply talking about themselves. Sympathy becomes too much moral responsibility for the hapless client, and he flees the bordello. "Not the absence of vice, but vice there, and virtue holding her by the throat seems the ideal human state," wrote William James in "The Dilemma of Determinism."

Tozzi is virtually unknown in English, and there is so much to explain about his artistic itinerary, and to explain all at once. Each bit of information seems as relevant as the next—one wants to cast a simultaneous blanket of information. Language itself becomes the primary obstacle to such simultaneity as well as the only means. Tozzi, too, was frustrated by literary construction, and by the notion that if you said one thing about a character or a scene, then you might inadvertently suggest that something else couldn't also be true. He defied such strictures by collapsing time and logic and by allowing characters to love and hate simultaneously and without apprehension. His writing, though the language itself is direct and simple, mimics a frenzy of emotion, despair, confusion and passion, destiny and hope. In his critical essays, Tozzi argued that each well-constructed sentence has the capacity to represent every aspect of the story simultaneously, and that a well-written piece of prose doesn't need to be read in linear order to be comprehended. Plucking sentences randomly from their context is a perfectly legitimate way of reading, and if a text falls apart under such scrutiny, then it isn't a text worth reading.

Tozzi defended the use of dialect: "Men who have had something to say have written well, precisely because writing well means being master of one's own intelligence and one's own sensibility. He who does not know the Italian language well enough should write in his own dialect, or at least, articulate his own syntax—not according to his ear, but according to the natural rules of his dialect." This was a position that led him to be characterized as a "local," or—more condemningly—"provincial" writer. In a discussion of the similarities between Tozzi and Giovanni Verga, his predecessor in realism and use of the vernacular, Alberto Moravia wrote that "neither Tozzi nor Verga simply used dialect—their work goes more deeply than dialect. They derive the life of spoken speech that makes speech more than just dialect, but also psychology at the unconscious level."

One might claim Tozzi is undiscovered—a neglected genius—that an ungrateful Italy, too fascinated by Futurism and Fascism, buried him in the dusty stacks of regional writers, landscape letters: *TOZZI, Federigo (1883–1920), see Siena, Sienese writers, Tuscany, dialect*. But that would be a half-truth. Tozzi's reputation did suffer, temporarily, during and right after World War II, a period in which realism turned outward to the political situation: the writers Cesare Pavese, Ignazio Silone, Elsa Morante, Primo Levi, and their counterparts in neorealist cinema—Luchino Visconti, Vittorio De Sica, and Roberto Rossellini. Taken in the context of World War II, the mysterious acts of man were no longer as benign as picking up a stone, and the emotional and intellectual contortions of simple, bourgeois life, no matter how ruthlessly treated and how true, seemed luxurious. In Tozzi's own time, art was meant to either transport the reader out of the mundane, according to Benedetto Croce's aesthetic instruction, or it was meant to challenge the reader, be fragmented, philosophical, difficult—eventually postmodern. At least that way, battle-scarred Italy felt it was working for its art. Peace has more or less settled over Western Europe, and since the late 1960s, critics have turned back to Tozzi with impunity and discovered what's challenging about his provincial realism.

In 1976, Moravia described Tozzi's world of prewar

Tuscany as devoid of ideology—"a static society that even in its stasis reveals incurable contradictions, where both immobility and longing for movement coexist." He defined Tozzi as a "physiological" writer, because "he feels life in the pain of the body before the pain of the soul. Tozzi's characters are continuously doing bodily things: they shudder, they faint, they vomit, tremble, cry, sweat, desire, refute, and so on. In the absence of an ideology to inspire and guide their behavior, his characters' obscure and unpredictable reactions most often spring from the body. Yet, when all has been said and done, it is necessary to emphasize that Tozzi's work, despite being corporeal and unpredictable, is one of the most exacting and astute portraitures of Italian society in those years."

Perhaps it was too exacting and astute for comfort. Critics didn't necessarily understand Tozzi's poetics when he was alive, and it is evident that they still hadn't understood them when Emma Tozzi wrote the preface to *Novale* in 1925. She clearly thought there were things about her husband's work that needed to be set to right: "Noting the uncertainties or inexactitudes made in recent newspaper and magazine articles, by those who are judging him based on his work, I realized that there's a need for people to know better Tozzi, the person. While all of the work comes out of periods of toil and struggle, value should be put less on his permanent spiritual reality than on what can be gleaned from his transitory psychological states of mind."

It's not easy to characterize what people thought of Tozzi in 1920—or even where he stands in the canon today. It would be impossible to pluck a familiarizing comparison out of the annals of belles-lettres—*Tozzi was a Tuscan Katharine Mansfield . . . a turn-of-the-century William Trevor . . . Italy's Kafka*. Even during the Tozzi "revival" of the last twenty-five years, the single most consistent theme has been regret that

Tozzi was never given his due. In encyclopedias, textbooks, critical studies, prefaces and introductions, the cant of self-reproach recurs. "Along with Pirandello and Verga, Tozzi is the major short-story writer of United Italy; and it is a serious limitation of the literary culture of our country not to have comprehended his greatness," wrote the critic Romano Luperini in his 1995 book on Tozzi. In 1968, the historian Gianfranco Contini wrote: "The standard estimation doesn't seem to meet the excellence of the results, for which it is perhaps too limited to consider Tozzi merely the best Italian writer of the twenties."

For good reason, critical writing about Tozzi tends to focus either on his biography or to analyze his actual psychology through his fiction. He wasn't a product of any Italian school or Continental movement, but wrote according to highly attenuated ideas about literature—its shape and purpose. He drew influences from world literature, classic texts, science, philosophy, religion. He plundered his own life, environment, and experiences for stories, inviting "subjective" criticism. His writing life was lamentably short, and yet he was a remarkably prolific writer—"He worked in a fury, with prodigious flow, filling page after page almost as if the words were being delivered to him by dictation," explained Emma. Critics and readers are left with a substantial body of work, but one that represents a discrete moment and barely hints at where his evolution might have taken us next. We have a burst of Tozzi—a mere twelve years of vigorous writing. But what a burst.

Minna Proctor

· LOVE IN VAIN ·

LOVE IN VAIN

■ ■ ■

Roberto Scandigli held a modest property in the country. His house faced Siena on one side and an endless road on the other. On the side facing the city, there were cherry trees standing as tall as the windows and a brook hidden among the oaks that ran down from a rocky mountain stream to the bottom of the slope and fed into a river, where the farmhands had built a little wooden footbridge.

The grapevines, their stems wound tightly around the stakes, had already been harvested and were losing their yellow leaves. A fat farmer with a black beard was leading a pair of bulls and a plough over the rough terrain.

Roberto Scandigli lived in the house year-round. Two peasant families lived in the apartments below his, and under them were the stalls where the pigs and horses were kept. Adjoining the house by the barn was the livery, its entrance barely wide enough for the carriage to pass through. Husks of maize and squashes being dried for seed hung from the crossbeams over the carriages.

In a little square, fenced-off area stood the chicken coop; and a pergola ran the length of the city side of the house, abutting the property line of the next farm.

There was an archway on the other side of the house that

served as the entrance to the living quarters, a second chicken coop, the laundry, and the basement. There were also two narrow sheds for coal and tools. Roberto Scandigli kept the keys to those rooms.

The façade of the house was decorated with faded mythological frescoes that two German artists had painted for Roberto's father: two young men, who had crossed half of Italy on foot and appeared at the door one day asking for charity. Roberto's father said: "Why are you begging?"

"We . . . painters are." And they showed him a portfolio filled with landscape drawings.

"Well then, I have some work for you."

And he brought them to this house in the country which back then was still in the middle of construction. They agreed to paint whatever he wanted.

The two Germans worked for a month. Then, fatter and cleaner, they snuck away.

The frescoes were dreadful; and time was like a sponge, blurring them and making them worse.

But Roberto's father, who knew nothing about art, was pleased nonetheless—in particular, because he'd spent so little on the project.

Roberto wanted to paint over the façade, cover the obscenity, but he never seemed to have any extra money. Every year, he decided he could put it off a little longer—until it became really intolerable.

In the meantime, he planted some climbing vines, which grew up over the frescoes, making them look as if they were always meant to just be trellises.

He planted daisies and chrysanthemums in little round flowerbeds that he had designed himself.

He planted two almond trees and five cypresses that he hoped would grow tall. He took some pieces of wood and painted them green, then built an arbor out of them for the grapevines.

But the time still hadn't come for him to take a wife. He was waiting for the house to get prettier and his farm more fruitful.

He couldn't imagine that a woman after his own heart, the kind of woman he wanted to find, would want to live there year-round in the company of farmers, unless there was at least a little rock garden where she could gather roses.

And he wanted to put pergolas all around the house, and make one very long in anticipation of the walks he would take with *her.* Another one would be round, with a comfortable chair, so his wife might sit in the shade while she knitted a pair of lovely, brightly colored slippers or made those elegant cushions—the kind he'd seen in the houses of the best people.

But the years passed relentlessly, and the pergolas still weren't finished. There was always so much other work to do in the fields—such obstacles to the realization of his ambitions!

Successful harvests were infrequent, and expenses were always enormous. Things didn't move forward as he wanted and had planned for in his dreams.

The first three years, he had the farmhands do his laundry, while he occupied himself with making the bed and sweeping up. Every other day a peasant woman would buy him a steak, which he cooked over the wood-burning stove.

Otherwise, in the evening he'd go to eat in a humble restaurant on the outskirts of the city. Some nights, he made do with fried eggs, salami, or boiled potatoes. He helped himself to wine from the casks, drinking without much concern for economy.

But he missed having a woman around and every so often

was struck hard by this obsessive desire. He waited impatiently for a nice girl to reveal that she loved him. Left to his own devices, he would never make a move!

And then, the daughter of a railway worker's widow let it be known to him, through another woman he'd been friendly with since childhood, that she intended to woo him. This flattered his ego, but he rejected her offer. The girl was rather homely. "If I'm going to take a wife, I want her the way I want her!" And he waited, waited in desperation.

In the evening, before going to sleep, he'd reflect on all the girls he'd ever seen. They were lovely girls, passionate and pure, just the way he wanted — maybe. One had a way of carrying herself when she walked, like a quattrocento figure in a painting he'd seen in a gallery as a young man. Another had a beautifully shaped head and the most perfect face. All those smiling lips, inviting him into chaste and eternal love.

Once he fell asleep pretending he was embracing the girl that most persistently appeared in his mind. Oh, how wonderful! How delicious a sensation! That night he dreamed of her, a sprightly nymph draping her hair over him. Her hair filled with grape leaves felt heavy on his body. Then the nymph fell asleep. And he lay there listening to her breathe, watching her breasts rise, her rosy skin, the dress he'd last seen her in. And he waited for her to wake, though her sleep was like distant music . . .

His big bed was like a desert. Sometimes he'd stretch out across it in search of a leg to squeeze between his own. He liked to dream of her in the morning, when he was only half awake, when dreams are more wonderful, because one is aware of dreaming and the images are more vivid.

He would feel like crying. He was so alone. The other pillow was untouched. He'd lay his head there, imagine he was going to find *her* body there. He would have hugged her tightly to his chest. For a month he almost believed a young girl was sleeping next to him. He'd reach his arm out nervously: a spasm that took over his entire being. Then he'd shut his eyes, thinking that inside that dark head of curls she was thinking of him too. One morning he asked aloud, "Did you sleep well?"—his delusion thus revealed to him in one cruel stroke.

He'd certainly go mad if he kept on like this! He was convinced of it. Any moment he would surely be tied up and carted away. In the meantime, his imagination swelled. Even the simplest gesture was accompanied by thoughts of his princess. He almost started feeling nostalgic for what he might have felt for her, had they ever been together. He dreamed of her daily habits, her smile. He didn't wash his hands or face until she was dressed, too. There she was: getting out of bed. He could hear the soft delicate sound of her feet on the ground. There she was: putting on her robe. He could hear the brush of the fabric. He called to her, asked her something. She left the room before he got up, went to heat up the coffee and milk; she brought it to him.

It was strange that when he did find her, he couldn't look at her; it was impossible. For what if she were to look back at him? One glance was enough. Those pale eyes hypnotized him. He walked on, ran his errands, gave instructions; and those eyes penetrated his soul. They lodged there, like two rabbits in a silent hole.

So why didn't she ever write to him?

She wasn't the only one he liked. Almost every girl had some distinction that made him desire her.

Walking up the road, he saw a young girl standing behind a large wooden gate. She wore a blue ribbon in her chestnut hair; her dress was cut low. That girl! She arched her neck so gracefully. And her head was elegant, like a crystal glass.

Another: when she walked, showed off the curves of her legs.

Another: had a sensuous mouth that seemed heavy with kisses, with beauty.

Another: wore red velvet around her neck and over her perfect broad shoulders.

His house, so bereft of the presence of other people, filled with the sweet dreams of his desire. An unreal beauty extended throughout, mounting with the exaltation of his spirit.

But the beauty wasn't connected to anyone, and when he recognized that, he would suddenly feel the pain of his situation. And then he would be overcome with a reckless love for everything beautiful. And everything is beautiful. He fell in love with the fields, the vines, and the animals.

He owed a visit to an elderly lady who had been close to his mother, and finally, without having foreseen it, his decision was made.

The lady had a daughter: tall, bony, altogether rather homely.

At the end of the visit, he said, "How much nicer it is here than at my house!"

He admired their big garden filled with flowers and the orchard with more than a hundred lemon trees. The house was spotless, the furniture dusted. The girl, Clotilde, was simple and domestic, almost awkward in the homemade dress she had cut and sewn with her mother's help. Despite their wealth, she wore a pale blue apron with little white flowers; her hair was poorly arranged, her barrettes stuck out more than they stuck in. She'd become slightly hunchbacked from all the sewing and didn't even seem to notice the strands of hair that fell out over her forehead and neck.

Her mother had decorated their rooms herself. Clotilde's had a low nightstand made out of painted cast iron. A votive candle was perched under a painting of the Madonna. There was a little table with an oval mirror, a few brushes placed with precision on top. Just a tiny bottle of toilet water shimmered brightly through the hazy air and against the broad expanse of wall.

At sunset, a ray of light, its color indefinable, streamed in over the clothes hanging on the wooden rack, reflected off a hairpin, bounced off the mirror; and then it was impossible to see the view out the window: just pale colors mixing with the light.

Clotilde stood behind her mother; her silence was friendly, hospitable.

Her mother punctuated every sentence with, "Come back to visit us soon! We never see anybody."

He answered, "I'll be back."

And he stayed away a month. During which time, his decision became evermore apparent. He resisted the voluptuous, provocative images of the nubile girls he'd never loved anyway. He forced himself to stay pure, to sharpen his will.

He had a vague sense of regret over the loss of his innocent fantasies. Oh, they weren't really gone! He could still see them, as if they were behind a distant veil—there, but less insistent. In his mind, he was convinced that Clotilde and her mother already knew of his decision; he didn't have the strength to disappoint them. More than once he set off in the direction of their house and turned back halfway down the road. Even the journey itself enticed him, beckoned him!

And when he received a basket of sweet-smelling lemons from Clotilde's mother, he thought, as he wrung his hands, *This is my chance! This is the right opportunity. I'll go thank her and . . .* But this presented another dilemma. Roberto didn't want the two women to think his gratitude was merely a pretext and that he'd been thinking about Clotilde for four weeks running. There was no room in his love for ambiguity. *They'll take me for an idiot. No! I'll show them that I still might change my mind. Not to think that I'm suddenly . . . giving up?*

To tell the truth, Clotilde wasn't overly concerned about whether or not Roberto was going to ask for her hand. Ever since they were adolescents, their marriage had been an ongoing project which their respective parents had discussed enthusiastically. Clotilde, so very reticent, clung to that vision, because it was something that would happen without effort, without fretting. It was the only conceivable love for her. She would have agreed to marry him without any excessive fanfare.

But his parents, who would have arranged the wedding as though it were any other occasion, died too soon. Yes, Clotilde's mother was still alive—hanging on to the dream—but the thread had worn thin; Roberto might yet compromise himself with another woman. And, as he never came around to visit, they weren't entirely sure he wasn't in love with someone else. So they decided to go visit him.

Thus they obligated Roberto to return the visit. It was a simple and polite way to tempt resolution. Women who have always dreamed of the same man cultivate a generous and innate habit of loyalty. They don't look elsewhere until they're sure they've lost their promised husband. At which point, they drown their passion and flaunt themselves just like any other woman; and their mothers end the negotiations—the last frontier of the perfect oblivion of youth.

In the best circumstances, such women become ideal companions, loyal like dogs, sure of themselves and of everything around them. What more could a man want than to plunder a woman's secret gaze without fear of what he might find there?

And so Roberto, after much reflecting over the pros and the cons, went to thank them for the lemons. Quite accidentally, he came across Clotilde at the head of the drive leading to her house.

Bad, he thought *It would have been better if I hadn't seen her first*. But Clotilde politely said hello, and he felt less embarrassed, his anxiety quelled. He began to observe how he felt when he was near her.

His soul turned violent: if nothing happened that very day then Clotilde was lost. After such a drawn-out period of agitation, you tend to move more easily in the opposite direction.

Clotilde's mother was waiting in the parlor. She'd barely greeted him; her hand was still wrenched in his grasp as he said, "So . . . I have come . . ."

There was no need to even say it.

Clotilde grew pale and fled the room. Her mother blushed, smiled, and looked surprised.

"Shall we discuss it more calmly?" she answered. And looked over to where her daughter had just disappeared, enjoying, perhaps, that she had disappeared so completely. Roberto didn't want to stand around and talk; he was so agitated he wanted only to run away. He couldn't look into the older woman's eyes—bright as they were, glistening with tears.

"So?" he asked, still gripping the woman's hand. She didn't answer. She started crying while still smiling. She seemed younger, and he didn't know what to do either.

Finally she called out, "Clotilde!" And through her voice flowed all of the intense gentleness of her soul. Her voice itself was almost soothing.

Clotilde didn't want to come. She was crying, too, stomping her feet and hugging the maid in a hundred different ways, and the maid, meanwhile, fluttered excitedly over her work in the kitchen.

All of it gave the impression of unpleasantness, an unpleasantness Roberto thought he would never forget. Clotilde's mother had to go to her, while Roberto stayed alone in the room. He perceived his head spinning, just a little, and he had to get over to the window.

Where everything had taken on the most peculiar aspect. A peasant woman passing under the window greeted him with a nod. He didn't respond, but was so touched by the greeting that he began to feel strangely light and invincible. His feelings came to the surface furiously, in bits and pieces. His heart beat convulsively. He could have cried for joy.

And he waited for Clotilde, who was putting on a better dress before making her reappearance. In the meantime, her mother came back in to keep him company, spinning — in every sense of the word — about the room, trying every which way to make the wait go faster. To no avail, he kept turning to her in the same moment she turned away from him to move a skein of cotton from the chair to the table, to shut a cabinet door.

Clotilde finally appeared. Roberto insisted on looking out the window when he heard her approaching footsteps. She went right over to him and hugged him. He turned suddenly and kissed her on the mouth.

On the way back home, he wondered why he'd been so idiotic as to kiss her right away. *It didn't feel the way I thought it would* . . . And he felt bound, too soon and without retreat.

He saw the girl with the thick, black, curly mane on the road. It was as if he'd lost her, and that made her seem even more beautiful.

He had to love Clotilde.

After that, his betrothed's kisses became more wonderful, more meaningful. With her he discovered the sincere security he needed in order to love. He turned all of his will over to her, as if it were too heavy for him to bear alone. On their wedding day, he didn't worry about their future. Over the course of their engagement, he'd forgotten his provocative fantasies and came to belong to Clotilde alone. No, she wasn't as pretty as he would have liked, and she had certain mannerisms that irritated him. But he had every hope that she would become perfect—the echo of his soul.

He thought her wedding dress was too tight, and he didn't like it. Clotilde did not have the elegance he'd admired in other girls. But he'd resolved to tolerate all of it until eventually she came to satisfy him in every way.

She had already given herself to him—in the attic, while her mother was busy in the kitchen, helping the maid. He suspected that she had given herself because she'd perceived exactly how little excitement she provoked in him. He hadn't been expecting such a gesture, and then he wasn't even satisfied by it.

Roberto had to resign himself to this limited and monotonous routine. He had the fleeting notion that he wouldn't go through with the wedding, and all the while, Clotilde was searching him out under the blankets, kissing him a little too much on his eyes, ears, lips.

Roberto lived with his wife in his house, and his mother-in-law stayed on in her own house.

But the pergolas still hadn't grown; what was there wasn't beautiful. And Clotilde concerned herself with other things around the house. By then, he'd begun to feel consumed by the destiny he'd brought on himself. Matrimonial love seemed too all the same and daily.

Nonetheless, he loved Clotilde enough, and she adored him.

And for three years he was faithful to her—a fidelity that

surprised him, made him happy. Clotilde groomed herself for him, bound to the instinct of possession which takes pleasure in simplicity. Moving only in accordance with the laws of nature, Clotilde could not be corrupted. Laws which are so logical and embedded regulate every human act. There is so much frank beauty in them; marriage becomes the most spontaneous and enduring fact of our basic desires. A sense of family grows, reveling in its own continuity. Why do you love your children? Because they are proof of devoted abnegation, the concession to which you've abandoned your vitality.

And the desire for more children comes out of the idealization of these sentiments—proof of the chosen condition. You kiss your wife for this, and her mouth becomes almost sacred.

Thus is the origin and evolution of families. No bond is stronger. And religion finds in it the stage for its manifestations.

Roberto perceived all this and was swept up in it. His love transformed itself to become an immense, inexplicable fact. That's why he married Clotilde—even if she wasn't at all like one of the young beauties who had once so conquered his spirit.

But after a violent attack of scarlet fever, Clotilde died. Which astonished and frightened Roberto. At first, he couldn't even bring himself to enter the room where her corpse lay among the lit candles, the perfume of flowers growing bitter, acidic as it mingled with the smell of putrefying flesh.

What a terrible stench!

He envisioned her: hands too small for her new gloves, her mouth decomposed, her forehead extruding, her cheeks sunken. Her eyes were spent coals.

Her stomach was so swollen they couldn't close the coffin. Finally in the cemetery chapel, the carpenter managed by brute force to secure the edges, sweating and frustrated because the ordeal took so long.

He thought of her for many long months. He couldn't pray, but he paid for the masses his mother-in law requested. He paid for all the bouquets of flowers she brought to the gravesite. But he could never bring himself to do the same.

Roberto grew very attached to a dog; he even let it sleep with him in his bed. Initially, he tried to keep the dog from lying on the side where his wife had slept; then he relented.

The animal followed him everywhere. It sat under his chair at dinner; he petted it in front of people; he let it lick his hands and chin.

Little by little, he returned to himself. He grew unhappy with his solitary life; his fantasies came back.

But the adorable women he had once smiled upon had grown old or had gotten married.

He didn't have the energy to find new ones.

Under his pergolas in the garden, he dreamed yet of the youthful, heady love he'd once felt for them.

(1910)

ASSUNTA

■ ■ ■

The big barn is drenched. The fog races from valley to valley, like a flag trailing in the wind, while the sun—wan but intense—hangs back, as if waiting to be born. The clouds lift, houses dot the hills, only to be hidden again by another mass of fog blown in from somewhere else. The landscape is swallowed up before our eyes. Here comes the wind, blustering in after the fog. It's left for the sun to penetrate this dense haze, to burst through the dark labyrinth, spread its radiance.

Oh, how the birds sing! As if wailing for their lost ones, bloodied suddenly against the blue background in the shadow of a trembling, overgrown poplar tree.

How they sing! Their voices ring thick as drops of water in this fog, with its tireless march forward, its retreat. The rain of invisible music. The secret way into our souls! Each note like a tear in a never-ending wail. Do they weep for the branches that too have been trapped in this fog? Perhaps. Their trembling, their fleeting songs, conjure up everything that could be obliterated by death. Perhaps. Life is veiled, then it's gone. And whatever follows the fog will be a sign of death. Our whole future lies in death, in death's greedy hands!

Finally the fog does lift, leaving but a few strips of itself, belts around the hills thick with vineyards. The sun is as hot as yesterday. Bees circle the old fig tree. Life has returned—sweetest and most eternal life. And then, from the wings of steel in the clear sky, with all its might, serenity and joy, the sun appears and fills the infinite horizon.

The barn dries quickly. Chicks and ducks can be heard. A shepherd ruthlessly drives his mule over the road leading to Pescaia. The sheep never stop bleating. Further up the road, oxen lead a caravan of ten carts up toward the city. The tall ladder leaning against the side of the shed throws a faint shadow. Husks of corn have been laid out on the roof to dry.

And the mountains are shrouded in a blue film. Except for Mount Amiata, which is drowned in the clouds.

Green shadows falling across the cornfields!

The light bouncing off the towers of Siena, making them shine white like chalk, an almost bluish white.

Marco came out to the barn, and the dog jumped up to meet him, putting its paws on him; the dog barked and then disappeared behind a pile of hay. Marco went to the goatshed and opened the little wooden gate to let the goats out.

Marco was the oldest son of one of the two peasant families that worked the farm. He had been in the army and been discharged six months earlier. His faded old beret bore the faint markings of his division.

But Assunta, the daughter of the other family, was still asleep—at least, he thought she was. Marco, who had been to the bordellos, and had long ago been corrupted by a big, fat farmer's wife, could now think of no one but Assunta, yet had to satisfy himself with consuming, secret fantasies.

He paused under the red archway of her bedroom window. Every so often he called softly to the straying goats.

To his mind the country was too slow. He wanted to scream, *Wake up! Come out and share this all with me!*

Hesitantly, he began to sing:

Blossom of acacia's thorn,
Everyone loves your mother
But I love you, love you more.

As he sang, the goats roamed the pasture. A few of them were swollen with milk, and their heavy teats batted against their legs as they walked.

There were white goats, black goats, and spotted goats. The hollow horns of the eldest were almost worn smooth where the tips had broken off. One goat stopped suddenly, then took off bleating and running, trying to catch up with the others.

Marco looked up at the house and wanted to sneak inside, to take his Assunta in his arms. After some time, a window opened and the girl appeared. Marco recognized the color of her dress.

She pinched a sprig of new basil from a plant. Disappeared for a moment, then just her arm reappeared to empty a bucket of water. Hadn't she heard him serenading her? Yes, maybe. But she pulled the window tightly shut after her. Mortified, Marco stopped singing. He figured out that there was no way Assunta could have heard him, because her window was too far up from the ground. And he fell even more deeply in love for having caught her at work when she didn't think anyone was watching.

He could see her red hair, smell its heady perfume. He stopped to listen, wondered if she was singing too. How greedy he was for her song! Her voice would echo his passion; it would be a fountain at which to quench his thirst.

But the shutters stayed shut. And Marco kept finding ways not to blame Assunta. He imagined hugging her, kissing her. Although she had never really cared for his attentions.

She didn't need him!

Her face was round and placid; and her red-ripe mouth rosewater sweet. That wasn't all. Assunta was an enigma of lust. Assunta made you think of one thing. Her neck, bared to reveal supple muscles, radiated heat. More than once Marco had undone the buttons on her dress, let it fall open to reveal her chest.

Assunta's laughter is sensual.

Marco loves her madly. Her wild spirit is wrapped in that peasant flesh. Her image appears in every one of his fantasies. He touches her calloused hands, he looks at her eyes, and a flame pulls him right into them.

When he thought about Assunta he was happy, even effusive. He'd greet everyone he passed on the street. He'd smile. He'd have the urge to talk with a blade of grass tucked between his lips. His Assunta! When her name came up, Marco's eyes would widen and grow soft with happiness.

That morning, the goats grazed eagerly. The quiet green pastures were like marvelous poems of simple love! The fields teemed with bugs and snakes, sounded with the songs of birds.

Assunta was a creature of that landscape.

As usual, Assunta was a little rude. Almost as if she wished he hadn't come. But he was persistent.

"Why don't you cut the grass over here?"

"It's longer."

"But I can't see you when you're over there."

"Does that matter?"

"I'll cut it for you over here."

And she seemed to grow taller.

"Give me the scythe," he said.

"But you don't know how to use it."

"I'm begging you, please, give me the scythe."

She pretended to be offended and shrugged her shoulders. Marco took the scythe from her hands.

"I'll let you do it only because that means I can nap on the grass over here."

Marco kneeled in the corn sectioned off for the animals. And no matter how much he suspected she was trying to insult him, he was still thrilled by the idea that she lay sleeping so close to him.

He wondered if it was purity that kept Assunta from abandoning herself to him. Then he chided himself, *I'm expecting too much.* But Assunta was truly bursting with all kinds of pleasure, as the pine tree is full of resin; because she dreamed of pleasure.

One man wasn't enough for her. She dreamed about being with all of them.

And she sat on the grass with her head in her hands, not once looking over at the man who wanted to marry her.

"Aren't you done yet?" She asked, sarcastic in her impatience.

"There's just a little left," he answered. He hurried to finish, breathing hard from the effort.

The goats had strayed.

"Are you going to bring it back up to the house?" he asked.

"Of course." She got to her feet and tossed him the rope.

He bound the bundle tightly, scraping his wrists in the process.

"What are you going to do at home?"

"I'm going to help my mother, and I'll be thinking of you." She laughed.

He was pleased.

The girl grabbed the small bundle and headed up the

road to her house. Marco stood between two staked grapevines and watched her go, following her with his eyes until she disappeared.

She arrived home and put down the bundle. She tightened the turquoise scarf decorated with red roses that she wore around her neck and called to her mother.

"The grass is here!"

"Come and do the dishes now."

She went, but without enthusiasm, dragging each step. When she reached the stairs, she saw Domenico sitting in the shade by the kitchen. He had been waiting for her.

Assunta blushed and put on a beautiful smile. Then, in a warm voice said, "You're here?"

The young man looked at her with cupid eyes and pinched her on the bottom as she passed on her way to join her mother at the pump. Her eyes flashed at him furtively.

"Am I supposed to wash dishes in this soup?"

"Use the hot water first, and dry them off too."

Assunta trembled with desire. It was if her flesh were shaking itself free of her clothes, leaving her naked and glistening. And her breasts in that moment, as if tempted to swell, made her head rush. She plunged her hands into the hot water.

Her mother was old. She had very dark eyes, and her skin sagged. She said, "Domenico, did you go to the market last Saturday?"

He nodded that he had.

"So, you didn't bring us anything?"

"Not even for me?" asked Assunta, turning to him, her hands steaming.

"Not even . . . for you." He answered with a smile. And he rubbed his blue eyes.

Assunta set the dripping plates on the table.

Her mother took a new dishrag from the drawer and handed it to her.

"I'm going out to take care of the rabbits," she said.

"Hurry back," answered Assunta.

The old woman put away the rest of the cups and left.

Then Domenico stood up. There was an irresistible sweetness in her eyes, and her mouth quivered just so. Her strong arms were bare to the elbows, and her fingertips were red. He grabbed her wrists and kissed her face with abandon.

At every kiss, Assunta smiled with surprising grace. She leaned back against the table in the pose of a woman surrendering.

"So," he murmured, "where?"

Her response was measured and distinct. She said, "Nine o'clock tonight. I have to go to Marta's. Wait for me at the bend in the road, by the high wall. I'll meet you there."

And she kissed him for the first time. Then she freed her wrists and turned back to the dishes.

Marco returned at noon. He was sweaty and tired. He saw Assunta by the entrance to the shed. The goats swarmed around her, bleating. A lamb, shut in the holding pen with its mother, poked its nose through the slats of the gate and watched the goats pass by. The lamb bleated too. It was still tiny, and its legs were too long. It hopped back to its mother's side.

"What have you been doing?" asked Marco.

"Didn't I already tell you?" She answered.

"You've been with your mother the whole time?"

"No . . ."

"Who else was there? Marta?"

Assunta was quiet.

"Nunziata? Your uncle?"

She wanted to laugh.

"Answer me!" he said authoritatively.

Assunta looked at him, vaguely irritated. He softened his voice and apologized. Then she answered.

"Domenico was here."

Marco led the goats into their shed. His heart pounded wildly with suspicion. He finished his work keeping his head lowered.

Domenico's face formed in his mind with devastating precision.

Assunta stood quiet and serious in the spot where he had found her. She wasn't looking out for his feelings.

After a quarter of an hour of silence, during which the only sound was the brush of the broom over the barn floor and Marco's heavy breath, she said, "Lovely roses."

"Where?" he answered instantly, his uneasiness making him feel small.

"Over there. Haven't you ever noticed them?"

Her face softened, and her lips parted in a smile.

He winced when he looked at her. Her beauty weakened him.

"They would look good on you here!" And he touched her very naked neck.

"Pick them!" she said, charming, impulsive.

"Give me a kiss, then."

"Just one?" And she gave him many. "So, go get me some."

"What if the owner sees me? They're in her garden, not ours."

"Then I'll ask someone else to pick them for me."

"Who?" he asked with concern.

"Won't you just pick some for me?"

He took the ladder and leaned it up against the pergola

covered with flame roses, and he picked quickly. "Is this enough?" he asked showing her the flowers.

She didn't answer. Marco liked the roses the more for the unbridled desire he imagined they inspired in her.

Marco picked another bunch, pricking his fingers. Then he dragged the ladder back to the barn and presented the flowers to Assunta. She gathered them in her apron and ran into the house. What did she do with them? Those roses were meant for her alone!

"Those are for us!" he called after her, his voice catching. But suspicion was already gnawing his stomach. Domenico's family was rich and very close to Assunta's.

How long did he stay? Marco wondered. *Were they alone together? Ever since I fell in love with Assunta, I never thought that he . . .* And a lewd image finished his thought for him. *But I'll have my revenge.* He sat down on an overturned trough. He felt in his pants pocket for his knife. Then, with even more clarity and speed than before, Domenico's face appeared to him. Marco contemplated the image angrily. There was fierce hatred in his eyes, across his brow. He imagined smashing Domenico's face with a stone.

The knife! The knife! The cry repeated silently in his head. Then he saw his rival stretched out flat on the ground, his shirtfront soaked with a bloody stain. *I'll stomp him, too.* Marco could feel Domenico's pulpy flesh under his heels. Then he'd bite him. He'd poke his eyes out with the end of a broomstick, slowly. *And for her?* He'd twist her arms and crush her breasts!

Then he'd ask forgiveness. The voluptuousness of her lovely, stupendous flesh overwhelmed him again. Every inch of his body cried out for her. *God! God, if you exist, make her mine! Make it so that I'm the only one she wants. Make it so that she'll never know the body of another man.* And love, more intense and more faithful than before, conquered him.

▪

Marco and Assunta didn't see each other very much the rest of the day and they sulked. He passed by her house several times again for no other reason than to see her. She was shut up in her room sewing.

Assunta's mother, otherwise occupied, spent the day away from the farm. Her wooden clogs, which Marco himself had made for her the previous winter, struck the cobblestones loudly as she walked off. From the henhouse, Marco kept watch. Assunta appeared at the window and then suddenly disappeared. When he was no longer at the henhouse, she started to sing, as if to call him back. She knew how to make him love her. His passion grew stronger every day. Who did she love? No one. Domenico was wealthier and nicer; she preferred him. Her thighs trembled when she thought of him. She dreamed of lying under him, his strong arms wrapped around her. And it wasn't a matter of feeling loved. Coupling got all mixed up in her mind. And her being was perpetually glutted with fantasy. She never tired. Pleasure reinvigorated itself in her with every rush of blood.

That's how she lived. What she surrounded herself with made her happy.

And everything yielded to her cool, supple flesh. She would have stripped in the wheatfield for every one of her admirers. The summer passed. She wanted everyone to want her. She wanted to feel all those hands on her body, she took pleasure imagining so many different faces looking down at her. And she was enervated by quantity.

To her, the sensation of coupling was infinite. Sweaty and rapt in fury, she craved caresses, and her eyes disappeared behind her lids. Only she knew where she went. And then she gave even more of herself, her longing unabated.

She had a beautiful body. A broad torso, a strong groove

running up her spine. Her waist was perfect. Her full breasts were firm. She thrust them out when she was alone, ran her fingers over them, her mind weak with flame.

That day her hips trembled relentlessly as if she were being chased. She allowed thoughts of Domenico to completely obsess her, and she couldn't wait for evening to fall. The pain of her imagination tightened around her neck. When evening arrived, the landscape seemed to grow wanton. She imagined the plants entwining limbs with the shadows. The country was in heat, as she was.

She told her mother, "I'm going over to Marta's until ten."

"Who's going with you?"

"Marco will bring me home."

"Go on then."

The old woman didn't seem too concerned. Assunta gestured to Marco, who was passing by on his vigil, and asked, "Come and pick me up at Marta's. But come after ten, because we have a lot to talk about and we're also going to mend one of my petticoats."

"Whatever you want."

She looked in his eyes as though she had the power to intoxicate him, and added, "What will you do in the meantime?"

To make her happy, he answered, "I'll stay here and keep your mother company."

Which made her suspicious: "Why?"

The old woman smiled, and Marco didn't understand. But he was worried he'd said the wrong thing, and his face clouded, nervous and upset.

Assunta's eyes shone. She hesitated, trying to figure out what Marco was thinking, but then she realized that he didn't suspect anything and hurried to leave. She wanted to avoid the usual questions and was blatantly rude to him so that he wouldn't insist on walking with her. How often could she avoid him using her friend Marta as an excuse? She smiled maliciously.

Marco, standing in the heat by the fireplace, looked back at her with a troubled and supplicating expression. He seemed horrified.

Marta arrived shortly to fetch her. She was young and honest, a good girl. Her golden hair framed her smiling face.

The two friends said good-bye and joined arms and left. Marco followed them to the doorway and stood in the twilight watching Assunta as long as he could see her. The day was extinguished by the sunset like a glowing hot iron in water. This painful day! What did it matter if the goats were shut up and starving. What did it matter if the calf's eyes implored another mouthful of corn. Everything had lied to him that day, even the sun.

If only the evening had the power to soothe him! If it could change something, carry his spirit out into the sweet blue, to where the stars twinkled!

A little bit down the road, Assunta told her friend, "I'm not coming over to your house. I'm going to meet Marco here by the wall . . . but my mother doesn't know. Go on without me."

Marta was hurt and jealous. She had wanted to talk about her boyfriend and show Assunta her silver ring. But she was an accommodating girl and answered, "There's someone closer to your heart than me. You're right."

Assunta was already pulling away.

"Good-bye," she said.

"Good night." Marta squeezed her hand. And then moved away, wrapped in the pale gleam of the full moon. The stars were innumerable, shining over the whole territory like silent fires, glowing gentle infinity.

Domenico emerged from the bushes on the bank across

the road. Without waiting, he kissed the girl and led her up to where he'd prepared a clearing.

They were hidden among the oaks.

Marco stood thoughtfully near the fire that by now was fading to ash.

All at once, he felt able to express things to his future mother-in-law that he hadn't even dared think before.

His hands trembled in the light of the fire. He spread his fingers out and watched them.

"I'm going to marry Assunta . . . you know. Do you still believe it?"

He needed the old woman to trust him.

"Do you still believe it? Answer me."

He was almost stuttering. But the old woman smiled, which he took to be a bad sign.

"Do you believe it? I won't say it . . . if you don't answer me."

"I believe it."

She had answered mostly out of curiosity, but still thought that his promise was useless, even though he repeated it every day and it made him happy.

"I'll marry her for sure . . . But she . . . did . . . Has she been talking to anyone else?"

It seemed like an enormous, impossible question. He was immediately sorry he'd asked it.

The old woman, on the other hand, had been expecting it for some time, ever since Marco had proposed to Assunta. She wasn't surprised at all. Nevertheless, she stayed quiet and stopped smiling. The lines on her face seemed to flatten out, as if another soul were being revealed. Marco sought in vain to find an answer in her face. Then she gave him the answer that consoled him, the answer he'd been looking for.

Assunta couldn't possibly be leading him on. The old woman had agreed to the marriage, and it was inconceivable that Assunta had been lying to both of them.

"I know . . . there's been talk . . ." he persisted.

"What can I tell you? Nothing has gone on here in my house!"

And again a great confidence washed over him.

"No, not in the house. No. But . . . people do talk."

"What do I know? I don't think she's capable. You're going to marry her."

"Yes, I'm going to marry her. And I want her to love me as much as I love her," he continued, emphasizing his affection.

"So? She loves you."

They both fell silent for a while. The old woman's breathing was labored. The lines on her forehead grew deeper and troubled. Her white head hung so! It seemed so heavy.

Marco was worried that he'd offended her.

"She's just always been a little silly. Don't say anything to Assunta about this," he said without reflection.

The woman looked up.

"I love her very much. You know that?"

The mother nodded and picked a spindle up from off its rack. She braced it under her arm, and in the glow of the lamp began spinning. The spindle moved up and down, following the wheel. She wetted two fingers on her lips and tended the fast, regular turns. He watched her without knowing why, in his mind all he could see was Assunta.

Suddenly he said, "I'm going to go pick her up right now."

Trying to keep him there, the mother answered, "Well, how generous of you! And leave me here alone to spin."

But he grew frenzied at the thought of seeing her. He exclaimed, "I'm going now! I'm going right now!"

She said, "Whatever you want."

Out of kindness he felt guilty toward the old woman, but from the moment he left the house, he was carried along by anticipation.

The moon hanging low was like a fire in the olive grove.

Along the road, he heard the sound of two lovers kissing. He smiled, thinking of the couple hidden among the oaks. In just a few moments, he too would have Assunta in his arms.

He quickened his pace.

Domenico heard someone passing by and didn't know who it was, but he got to his feet and opened his knife.

The girl behind him lay still, sprawled on the ground.

Marco could make out two distinct shadows. And in the distance beyond, he could already see the light in the windows of Marta's house. When he arrived, he stood outside and listened. He heard Marta's silky voice mixing with the voice of her younger brother.

"Assunta!" he called.

"She's not here," answered one of Marta's brothers.

Marta emerged in the doorway holding the oil lamp that she had taken from the mantel of the fireplace. She didn't hide her surprise, suspecting nothing.

"Isn't she with you?" she asked. Then anxiously fell quiet. Had she betrayed her friend? She felt troubled.

The young people called out to Marco to come inside, but he was already disappearing into the shadows.

The flame from the light shined thin like a razor.

"Good night!" he said.

Marta stood in the doorway until her brothers pulled her back inside, and they all started talking about Assunta and Marco.

Marco ran back to where he had heard the love-making before, but the clearing was empty now. He wanted to touch the leaves spread on the ground, as if they would prove something. He bounded up the road.

His soul was twisted in terrible confusion. His temples were swollen and throbbing. It had been her! Within moments, he was back in the kitchen at the farm.

Assunta was sitting there.

"Where did you come from?"

She turned pale and tried to smile. Marco repeated, "Where did you come from?"

"Wasn't she at Marta's?" asked the old woman.

"No," answered Marco.

"Where were you?" asked the mother, heedless in her questioning of the ugly consequences. There are some moments when we are sincere without meaning to be.

Assunta got up to leave the room, but stopped suddenly and started crying, believing that she had been discovered.

Marco was just two steps from her. She wondered if Marta had told on her! And she felt as if no one, not even her mother, was protecting her. She abandoned herself to destiny.

But she wasn't crying out of pain or regret. She was crying in anger, because she'd gotten caught and felt powerless against what they were going to say to her. She wept loudly so that Domenico would hear her.

"You!" screamed Marco.

"What did she do to you?" asked the mother, who still hadn't fully understood the situation. Then, Assunta thought she might find some refuge, however weak, with her mother. And Marco took the old woman's incomprehension as evidence.

He was, even in his wild confusion, a picture of naïveté.

"Who were you with? Who!" he screamed. "Say it! Say it!"

His rage seemed strange even to him. But he still thought he might be wrong and would have to cry and beg forgiveness. Assunta had figured it all out, which made her less frightened, so she stopped crying. Now she was bracing to defend herself, to lie again. But that made things worse, because Marco, driven to the extreme edge of his nature, would not stand for any more hesitation. Her deficiencies became real, manifestations of the south wind. His love was a field without truce.

"I'll kill you. I'll kill you!"

Assunta cowered behind her mother.

"I know it was Domenico. It was him . . . Or, who?"

The girl, shaken by tears, looked like she was going to fall to her knees.

"Are you going to tell me?" Then, turning to her mother, he said, "Don't defend her if you are innocent. Don't let her influence you."

Assunta was surprised by his audacity. She never would have imagined him to be capable of such resentment. She weakened for a moment. But pulled herself together and answered him evenly, "Yes. I'll tell you."

"Who was it? Who was it?"

"You said it yourself already."

"Domenico?"

"Yes . . ."

He punched her in the face, then kicked her to the ground.

Assunta screamed, and her mouth twisted. Her mother was frightened and rushed out to call the neighbors. Marco knelt down to strangle the fallen girl. How the fascination of her beauty had disappeared!

He was already squeezing her throat with both hands. Her eyes bulged and popped out from her face. They stared up at him horribly. All of her hatred married to a spasm of death. Even the terrible contortions of her face communicated a vendetta without limit.

He let go suddenly. But it hadn't been enough. He needed to push harder and quickly! Her dry throat closed. Her head lolled, her body convulsed and twisted uselessly, her bones made dull thuds against the kitchen floor.

If she could have asked for pity? If her hands had clasped in a plea? But instead they pushed in vain against the man crushing her. And death struck her as a disgusting kind of lust, one without pain.

"Let her go!" screamed Domenico appearing out of nowhere. Marco leaped to his feet.

"You will pay," he cried, as he recognized Domenico through his convulsions, and seeing a knife, grabbed it and plunged it into his heart.

Domenico fell, knocking his head against the table. His expression changed; his face contorted.

Then it seemed to Marco that all things present fell on him.

He observed the pool of blood and was frightened. He didn't think again of Assunta, who seemed to have lost consciousness. He fled from the farmers who were now running toward the house from the other side of the barn.

(1908)

FIRST LOVE

■ ■ ■

Emilia told her beau, "I'm going to get milk for the teacher. I'll be right back."

And he answered, "I'll wait for you."

They exchanged almost the same words every evening when they met in the piazza of San Domenico. Then, without stopping with him, she'd disappear through a wooden gate, behind which bundles of corn and millet were piled for the cows.

The sunset shimmered behind the stall.

She came back after a quarter of an hour. They stood in silence for a long time. She shook her hair across her shoulders. He looked at her, but didn't know what to say. Her silent, smiling mouth almost seemed insulting. Nevertheless, his body coursed with involuntary sensuality.

She laughed at him, her eyes shining.

Finally, Giacomo asked, "Couldn't you have come earlier?"

She blushed and answered, "The teacher doesn't let me out earlier."

"And now you're going back to school?"

"Yes, and then home. Wait for me by the door. Why didn't you follow me last night?"

"I didn't follow you?"

"You disappeared. You were in a very serious mood."

"I don't like not being able to see more of you."

"I'll walk more slowly tonight."

And they touched fingertips.

He didn't understand why he had to walk behind her to her house. Maybe it was because she didn't want him. But those brief encounters, in the twilight off in the corner of the piazza, worked him up.

In the mornings, she used to walk by his house. She would take the long way round to get to her lesson. And he'd press up against the glass panes, waiting for her, so he wouldn't have to risk opening the window.

Giacomo couldn't say for sure what color her eyes were. (They were blue.) He saw only her soul and felt the mysterious rapture of a young girl's body. He thought a lot about her mouth, which inexplicably seemed to be a sign that she loved him.

But why had she responded to his love?

Giacomo had first seen Emilia at a town fair. Through a crowd of people, he saw her looking out over the streets, its arches illuminated by tiny white and red lights. She was with her mother. He only glanced at her and was rewarded with a surreptitious glance in return. But back then, he hadn't really expected her to reciprocate his love.

He came home drunk that night and told a friend, "I've found love!" He was dizzy with youthful ecstasy which was expressing itself for the first time.

One day Giacomo told her, "I'm alone in the world. My mother died five years ago. And what will I do if I lose my father, too?"

He was on the verge of tears. Emilia answered, "I'm here, aren't I? I'll keep you company."

And he thought, *You? I'm ashamed of you. I don't like you. I don't believe you.*

She was vexed by his silence and scolded, "If you're not going to leave me, why won't you tell me that you love me?"

Then, since he didn't say anything, she continued, more agitated now, "You shouldn't talk like that."

But he revealed that he was in even greater pain, completely undone by this terrible nightmare. His distress, though, came from the state of mind he alone had worked himself into. He had the idea that this feeling of love had made him uncommonly melancholy and given to moments of panic in which his spirit flailed beneath the weight of enormous stone wings.

Then Emilia smiled sweetly.

Why is she laughing? he thought. *Am I so ridiculous?* And he attempted in vain to appear indifferent.

"We haven't ever kissed," she said suddenly.

Kiss you? But your lips scare me. And I'm not attracted to them. I'll not give you any kisses. Nevertheless, he moved closer to her face and kissed her out of curiosity.

But what is love? he thought. And he blushed because of the feelings he had for a woman.

He wasn't concerned with finding out whether Emilia was as innocent as he was, or if she were hiding some instinctive wisdom behind her words. He didn't wonder to himself if she was already an expert in emotions.

He had grown up in his father's house and had an aversion to all women.

But Emilia was more disposed to gentle impulse. Her married sister lived with her and their mother, who was a widow.

It seemed that she found frivolous perversions in other people's experiences, which urged her toward precocious love. Maybe it was the tenderness of those adolescent dreams—dreams that run like rivers off the flesh—that made her less hesitant. Why shouldn't she be allowed to love too?

She had let precociousness blossom; it was only naïveté. Mostly, the feelings grew out of pure, inexpressible sensations.

But passion seemed to drift through her eyes like a person who walks but doesn't know the road.

Finally, they managed to spend a bit of time together. But they didn't have anything to talk about. Suddenly, she laughed.

"Why are you laughing?"

"I just felt like it."

They walked quickly through the crowd, almost as if running from their feelings. Maybe they should have picked another place to meet.

"Everyone is looking at us," she said. "Someone will recognize me."

"What if they tell your mother?"

They tried to walk more casually, but the moment one of them drew nearer to the other, their sense of calm disappeared. Then, he stopped and looked at the silver bracelet around her wrist. And he couldn't think of anything else. Emilia thought that he desired her, and she lowered her eyes.

They parted without saying good-bye.

And then, while he followed her home, he was suddenly struck with the image of her impoverished family, all living in the stench of that dark house.

Emilia's sister was pregnant. She was tall and pale and leaned on her husband, who was a carpenter with a gaunt face and a prominent Adam's apple. Giacomo had often seen them with Emilia. Her mother was as peevish as she was old.

She had black eyes and a big head. Giacomo's love was fated to die with adolescence. This groundswell of foreign urges could not possibly continue with such vigor. This fleeting sweetness would be extinguished like a torch in inexperienced hands. Out of necessity, these two spirits would never come together. They would remain inside their selfish shells, more concerned with their own blithe maturation. Adolescence is lost under veils that grow heavier as time accumulates behind you. Sometimes you can find it again, but just barely!

Giacomo didn't show up for their regular date one evening. And the next day he ran into Emilia, who had been looking for him.

He gestured to her that he wanted to talk. But Emilia didn't want to listen. She rushed into her teacher's house.

So he got angry. And yet, a week later, he went to meet Emilia again in the piazza. She started crying; her face went red and wet with tears.

"Why are you crying?" he asked irritably.

She didn't answer.

"Why? What did I do?"

Emilia, worried about seeming unfriendly, made herself stop crying.

"Is it my fault?"

She blushed and wanted to leave, but he kept hold of her hand.

"Let me go!" she cried.

"Whatever you want," he answered sarcastically.

Then she said, "Let's stay together for a little while. My mother found out about everything."

Giacomo felt a pang.

"She made my brother-in-law whip me."

"And your sister?"

"She couldn't protect me. But she doesn't care about anything anyway."

"Why not? Doesn't she love you?"

She laughed, and said, "She only thinks about herself."

"So why don't I ever see you anymore?"

"You know why. I've been looking for you everywhere. I kept going by your house."

"I've been very busy."

"I'll say good-bye now."

"You're leaving so quickly?"

"Mamma's waiting for me at my teacher's house."

He grew angry. *I'll never talk to her again.* And, feeling a little downcast, he watched her as she turned to leave. Then, out of curiosity, he followed. But he tried to keep her from seeing him. He didn't want her to think he loved her.

And then he stopped caring. The whole idea of feeling for someone else seemed ridiculous to him. *Anyway, I don't really know her that well. I could say that I met her at a party. It was an accident. That I didn't look back at her because she loved me. I liked her for a minute.* He couldn't understand why two people would lock themselves up in mutual affection. The idea almost disgusted him.

After three weeks, a relationship with a woman seemed to him like a bad habit.

Another month went by, and they didn't see each other. Then he wanted to talk to her. But Emilia didn't want to talk to him. Giacomo felt so resentful, he wanted to beat her.

And yet, as time passed, his passion became affectionate again, and he almost longed for Emilia's embrace. He could clearly see then the inadequacies of their love. *I never loved her,* he told himself. *I never felt that communion with her, that sense of trust which unites two people. Did I lead her on? Why would she have wanted me to love her anyway?* When Emilia's face appeared to him, it was like the face of a stranger.

By chance, they saw each other again in a church. She avoided him, leaving through one of the side doors. He watched her walk away with a feeling of compassion. For she seemed to him even more beautiful.

(1908)

MAD FOR MUSIC

■ ■ ■

Through the observation of the typical characters you might come across, especially on the streets of small cities or towns, you can greatly enrich your understanding of life. There are those who—by the grace of fate's outrageous excesses—manage to set themselves apart from social norms. Yes, they may be exceptions, but don't they still represent a true, genuine aspect of human psychology? Aren't they worthy of our curiosity? If only for the pity they evoke?

We should study them attentively and thereby discover the inexplicable meaning of life. Yes, their ways strike us as more mysterious than our own, inscrutable even. But though these exceptions might be considered ignoble, they are still interesting and amusing.

I offer an example of one such exception.

At twenty-two years of age, Roberto Falchi was struck with a terrible case of meningitis and lost all trace of intelligence.

What became of him? He abandoned his second year of study at the technical institute and took up wandering, keeping company with other vagabonds. He never had a thought of his own again. His costumes and that idiotic expression plastered on his face made people feel kindly toward him and intrigued by him.

His father, a policeman, left him alone. Though he never entirely gave up on him. It had become clear that Roberto would not ever be able to return to school—this much the doctors had assured them. But wasn't there always the possibility of some kind of change—even a gradual shift—that would reverse the effects of the disease? He had always been a good young man, and he had studied hard. There was still time.

And Roberto Falchi walked up and down the streets, snacking on dried fruit and roasted chestnuts which he ate from a package tucked into his jacket pocket. He wasn't very nice to look at, and he was filthy, too. His socks were faded and baggy around his ankles. His face was pointy and his mustache was spare. His pale eyes were like the eyes of a dead fish. He smiled like an animal, wide open and compassionate. He made friends with people who, like him, didn't have anything else to do.

After many months of walking, he announced that he'd chosen a career; he would study music.

His brother was still at the technical institute and was about to go into the army. His sister was training to be a teacher.

Roberto Falchi spent his days smoking cigars in a café, never taking part in either the conversations or the games. He sat in the least crowded corner of the room, letting his drink get cold in its cup, surrounded by a cloud of smoke. The smoke was like his eyes.

He didn't seek out company; his friends would come to his house looking for him, or they'd find him out on the road.

He helped his mother with work around the house—he'd run the errands that normally the maid would have done. His books, fifteen or sixteen of them, sat in a pile on the end table in the living room. Upon deciding he was going to study music, he became obsessed with a bandleader from a nearby village. The bandleader had a massive head, the features of a peasant, and he was cross-eyed. Roberto learned the fundamentals of reading music from this man.

Then he bought a cheap mandolin and would play chords on it, humming along under his breath.

"Why do you have to sing along?" asked his mother. "Can't you hear you're tone deaf? It spoils the sound of the instrument."

He'd laugh, but he didn't agree with her and would hide his head in his hands.

Even his father participated in the discussions about his future.

"You'll become a musician all right. But you're going to starve to death."

Roberto blushed and was flattered.

His sister stood thoughtfully to one side, watching him play with an ardent expression in her eyes. His brother leaned straight as a board, his spine against the wall. He wasn't particularly interested in art. He would be a modest citizen. Anyway, it was only five months before he'd be going off to the army. His white, almond-shaped teeth gleamed between thin lips. His features were almost feminine; and he had perfect ears—though his forehead was sloped.

"Oh, he'll be a great musician!" he said, pointing at Roberto. And he laughed, too, with kindness and generosity.

Then the performer, who had a stutter, managed to get out several partial exclamations. And the mandolin trailed along, a light, silly sound.

Everyone was happy.

Roberto Falchi's best friend was an eccentric who wrote a book or two a day. His name was Niccolo Sfondi, and he was the son of a clerk from the tax collector's office. He had also fallen short of receiving his diploma from the vocational school and lost his mind two years earlier. He went through reams of paper, filling the pages with delirious ramblings.

A deep friendship developed between these two, each one deeming the other a genius.

They went out together every day, pausing in front of the smokeshop to read the newspaper headlines displayed in the window and discussing their thoughts.

Niccolo was not only a poet but claimed also to be a philosopher and a painter and a critic and a scientist, not to mention a very active member of the local gym. Both of them were so blessed with ignorance that when they appeared, they lifted the spirits of many people. And since it was a small city with a lot of gossip, they earned prominent reputations. There were two, even three, lawyers who kept track of their movements in their daily logs.

The two men kept to their paths, driven by their mutual confusion.

The musician was intoxicated by his popularity, by the people staring at him. But he was modest and didn't like to leave the house before dark.

And then, hands tucked into the pockets of his jacket or pants, he would endlessly walk up and down the main road, where all the girls in search of husbands gathered, along with the other locals. He'd head right down the middle of the pavement, his face lowered and shadowed by his broad, round hat. And he would hum arias from his operas to come. When people gathered at the municipal bandstand to hear music on Sunday afternoons, he'd stand off to one side and listen.

If an organ grinder happened to be passing through the city, Roberto would follow him everywhere. He'd listen to every performance. He also stopped to listen in the doorway of any shop where there was a phonograph playing. Then he'd set off again, walking and singing, his voice subdued and racked with the labor of composing a melody.

With his other friends, he scarcely said a word. When he needed to talk to them, he was formal and always left the decisions up to him.

"Which way should we go? Up the street or down?"

"Wherever . . . you want!" he'd smile, and spread his arms wide.

He didn't know any women, and he would blush shyly when the others talked about them and stand off to the side. Three years passed like this, and Roberto remained loyal to his rituals. He left the house late, walked the same path, made the same small talk, and then returned home.

Then, after this period had passed, Roberto introduced a pleasant change. He got up earlier in the morning and went to the pharmacy. He'd sit on a stool by the entrance and read the entire newspaper. Every now and then, he'd exchange a word with one of the shopkeepers. He'd leave finally, numbed by the activity, and hum as he walked home.

His brother was drafted and sent away. His sister became a teacher, and his father retired. Roberto remained the same.

But his clothes got worse. His old overcoat didn't even reach his knees; it was badly cut and badly mended. This shapeless coat seemed to make his face more repulsive.

And his mania intensified. When he walked, he'd wave his hands around as if he were a conductor; he sang louder now and more often.

To make matters worse, his best friend, the writer, had to flee Italy after being arrested and found guilty. Roberto Falchi became more gloomy. He'd only speak to friends of the hapless poet, harboring memories of the lofty discussions they'd once had—discussions that were so different from those he shared with anyone else. His belief in this difference was so great it took the form of an idiotic smile he always wore on his face.

"So, when can we expect an opera from you, Signor Roberto?" someone would ask.

He'd grow pale and wouldn't answer immediately.

"When can we hear something?"

He'd stutter and exclaim, "I . . . I don't know. I hear it coming to me from above," and he'd turn his ashen pupils upward. "But then . . . I don't have any pretensions . . . Fate will decide for me." And he smiled with satisfaction.

"Well then, enjoy your walk."

Roberto Falchi would move away from the crowd feeling miserable about the exchange which he perceived as ridicule at his expense.

His father was pleased about Roberto's career. He paid the teacher in advance for two years and arranged it so that his son could take as many lessons as he wanted to. His mother was so ridiculously attached to her son that she was fulfilled by the modest performances he put on for her. The whole family was convinced he had a great future.

"When my Roberto is famous . . ." Signora Falchi would say.

And he'd smile at her through his incurable illness.

There was a long period during which no one saw him. He suffered a very serious chest infection. And when he reappeared for his walks, his face seemed the worse for it.

Often, he went walking around the monastery, though he could never bring himself to speak to anyone and the monks watched him with disdain. That made him mad, and his mournful eyes grew agitated. He'd retreat like a dog.

When he passed someone on the street who he profoundly respected, he'd hum louder—ever trapped in insanity.

Some days, his face was cloaked in sadness, as if the heaviness of it all were breaking him in two and dragging down his pace. His eyes brightened a little when he'd happen past the lawyer who had been a friend of the poet. He'd almost tremble with joy. But he wouldn't risk greeting the man. No, instead he affected, as best he could, great indifference. And the lawyer would pass by without stopping. Then Roberto Falchi would turn to watch him from behind . . .

This lawyer was well respected in the city for his notable accomplishments. Right out of high school, he'd written a libretto that someone who worked in the post office had then set to music.

He was so well thought of that, though quite young, he held a seat on the city council.

He didn't know anything about music, which was why he was such a great admirer of Roberto Falchi, and he was secretly jealous of his friend the poet's pedestrian verses. Yet it was said that he would surely be elected mayor of that very city when he was older.

Roberto Falchi went to the public library, too, and he'd ask to see the works of ancient philosophy, though he didn't know how to read.

At the library he befriended a decorator who was crazy about the work of Jules Verne.

It wasn't uncommon to see him walking down the main street carrying a seed basket or watching a servant girl smile at a soldier. On summer evenings, he could always be seen standing on a corner by the barracks listening to the band.

The beating of the drums thrilled him; they made him feel light-hearted. And the strident tones of the trumpets made him think of grand opera.

That was the way he lived; and the way he still lives.

(1908)

SISTER

...

"The whole dark past reappears at the bottom of my soul, like a grinning corpse. And I feel like I came here running across a distant meadow, I am so tired. My energy has been squandered in contemplation. But I can remember having loved once, too."

Vincenzo fell silent after speaking these words.

The October mist heightened his pain. He was almost in tears as he met his sister's gaze. Then he grew less reflective. These emotions were too painful.

If I were to talk, would she understand me? In fact, Viola seemed liked a stranger to him. *We have the same mother.*

The tender greenness of the cypress saplings touched him. Dampness trickled off the russet bark. She asked him, "Where did you meet her?"

"Why are you asking me about her? All I remember is that we met once in a church in Arezzo, in front of the Piero della Francesca frescoes. After that my feelings turned impetuous. That was years ago."

Viola offered her hands, so slightly emaciated. There was dead passion hiding even behind the darkness of her eyes.

At which point he felt great sympathy for her. He felt their friendship binding them together.

"You've been in love, too?" he wanted to ask, but he didn't want to cause her any pain. He imagined she might cry.

"How did you lose her?" she insisted.

"My past is no longer mute; my affection has been resuscitated in the clouds. I can only produce sighs in the face of such memories."

The vehemence of his emotions turned to anguish.

"When will you ever feel such joy again?" she asked.

"Soon, especially now that I know it's what you want for me."

So that she doesn't have to feel sorry for me. He discovered tranquility in Viola's expression.

The path led past the elms. On the far side of the white stone benches, women strolled arm in arm.

"Shall we walk?" he asked. "Why should I let the past consume me?"

She smiled and felt just as gloomy as he did.

It was as if his entire past life were pounding his head with a stone. He shuddered spastically with fear and was worried his sister might realize how crazy he'd become.

It was true: his soul needed to love again. But who was out there for him to love? There were moments he almost convinced himself that all was lost. His soul was like the sculpted black marble of an old cathedral façade. He turned to look at her.

What kind of girl could satisfy him? Viola guided him back to the villa. It was an old building, almost in ruins, nestled in the oaks and the fir trees on the crest of a foothill. The windows looked out over the valley's lush curves and the perennial solemnity of the mountains: how the mountains lay in wait for the sun to go down in order to mount their stunning moment of beauty. They waited in sublime silence, wearing big green smiles. Flocks of birds rushed down off the mountaintops, setting a collision course for the nearby olive trees.

He had arrived late in the day. Voices floated out over the solitude and became music. A peasant's bonfire could have been part of a ritual to faith renewed.

He had spent several days in retreat. Viola kept herself occupied with the business of the house and closed herself up in the living room where all the books were.

She'd take her brother out in the morning or the afternoon, but he still wasn't getting any better. He had moments of ecstasy in which everything he saw seemed to be part of his interior experience. And he would suffer profoundly over something that had nothing to do with him.

"Why don't you write to one of your lady friends?" she asked. "You must be crying yourself to sleep every night."

Four men in white hoods passed by carrying a coffin on their shoulders and turned to look. He couldn't bear the gaze of those unknown men. The handles of the coffin jangled against the side. An old man and some women brought up the rear. The passing of death in the midst of all that green distressed him. *Why do they have to pass this way?* he wanted to ask. And he was repulsed by the glow of the torches between the hedges.

"You are so miserable," she said.

His sister wore a peaceful expression of intimacy.

"Why can't I be like you?" he answered.

An old woman came up to them begging for money. He stared at her while she thanked Viola. He wouldn't have given her anything.

The next day he told his sister, "I don't know why I'm staying here and burdening you with my misery. I think I'm a drain on your happiness."

"No, Vincenzo dear. I just wish I could do more for you. It pains me that I don't have more to offer you."

Then he recalled the power his sister had once had over her own mind. She was like a fresh mountain spring

But now? He had no idea what she'd been through over the course of their separation. He had been deeply in love and remembered nothing but that. She might have suffered for love, too. Experienced that pain for which there is no cure. Viola had aged. The skin on her face was more wrinkled than before. Her eyes were sunken with mystery. Her bosom had hollowed out. Her arms grown thin. And her brow seemed almost scarred with disillusionment, marked with destiny to be always alone and always sad. But she was strong. She could not have faked the peace and quiet of her everyday life. This life of tranquility was an adaptation that she'd made.

She should have been rich for her capacity for love! He could see by her eyes that she had forgiven someone's wickedness. And yet her chestnut hair seemed to be preserving the wounds of struggle and desperation. And it was her own pity that consoled her when she spoke of this person. He could never leave her all alone again.

His sister perceived that Vincenzo had come to a realization. That his eyes were full of goodwill and limitless devotion. Then she touched his hand and explained, "We are so brave!"

Everything pure about nature appeared to Vincenzo enclosed in the diaphanous vessel of the morning.

He asked himself, *What good does love do me? There is so much beauty, even in creatures we don't communicate with. Impossibility is its own temptation. Human life is too fleeting, it is like the dream of a god in the forest. Perhaps there is another faith. I will be her soul.*

But then it occurred to him that the friendship his sister

could offer wouldn't be enough; and he began to have doubts about his conclusions.

The murky need for a lover was brewing inside him.

Sometimes he suspected he was too weak — destined to lose his mind. He thought destiny was holding him by his impotent wrists and shaking him hard.

Meanwhile his genuine esteem for Viola kept growing, and he abandoned himself to the support she offered.

But how much can she take? I'm afraid I'm getting too wretched. He began to wonder if he stayed in his sister's house this intolerable condition would ever go away. *Wouldn't it be better for me to find solace with a woman?* He considered not discussing it with Viola, because he didn't want the conversation to change her disposition toward him. But he couldn't possibly leave without telling her. She should know his state of mind. He should say good-bye.

Viola found him deep in his reflections, sitting on an old stone chair.

"How are you feeling today?"

"I feel better."

He got to his feet and walked with her. The morning light grew long and threw stripes on the ground between the cypress trees. Warm sweetness fell from the sky.

"I want to *adore* someone," he said.

"And why shouldn't you? You can go."

"And leave you here alone?"

"You can go back to the one who wants you."

He became upset. Perhaps she didn't realize it, but he worried about causing her useless pain. Especially since he was so scrupulous. The thoughts raced through his head: *Who will be the woman I fall in love with? I already feel more than I ever have for her. As if my whole being is ready for her. As if my whole being were lunging toward her. I will be happy.*

(1908)

L'AMORE

■ ■ ■

The cloudy morning brightened, but the sea remained pale. Virginia Secci had already begun her morning walk and was moving slowly out along the wooden plank of the pier toward the posts at the far end. I watched her from the window of my house, just a few yards from the beach. The sails on the nearby boats were yellow and orange, while the boats in the distance seemed to have taken on the color of the sea itself; almost white.

I never once took my eyes off Virginia, because I was in love with her, and I was so very sad. I didn't even feel like leaving the house. Every time I looked at her, I became sad like that — maybe because I loved her too much. I would have liked to whisper dear and innocent words to her, although I'd have to keep an eye out for her husband. But I loved her despite him and was incapable of renouncing this long-held desire.

That's why I waited for her to return from her walk. In the meantime, I liked to reflect on the naïve, sweet, tender things I never said to her.

When she walked close to me — as she was forced to, because I had planted myself on the front stoop of my house, and she lived in the house next to mine — I was overcome by a familiar, heady sensation and didn't even acknowledge her as she passed, although I watched her. I felt myself grow white and, after having met her eyes, shifted my gaze out to the sand. I listened to her footsteps fade.

If I had a voice equal to my thoughts, I would never be afraid to speak. But I don't have an everyday voice, a voice I use with everyone, to speak about anything.

As usual, after having seen her, I locked myself inside the house.

Through the half-closed shutters, light reflections off the waves beat brightly across the wall and down to the floor — like mobile, weightless mirrors.

I looked out the window again in the afternoon, though I was almost certain I wouldn't see Virginia a second time, and the pain I felt was surly and vague like the face of her husband.

While I was standing there, the sea turned a deeper turquoise, making the sky even paler than the water.

Long strips that were almost white ran across the water, reaching all the way to the beach; then they disappeared.

I couldn't remember how long I'd been in the town of Cattolica. Maybe I was convinced I'd only just arrived. If Virginia had talked to me, I would have told her I loved her.

The sky was entirely gray the next day, and it had rained those last hours before dawn. The sea was green at the shore and purple toward the horizon. I didn't see Virginia. I don't know why, I almost believed I would be able to forget her. But that evening, I couldn't settle down because I hadn't seen her all day.

I was prepared to invent any excuse that would take me to her house — because even finding out she had suddenly died would torment me less than this. But a storm came, a mighty gale blowing up from Rimini. Many of the fishing boats returned to the harbor, moving painfully, in single file, up the winding stream called Tavollo.

That night I couldn't sleep and I promised myself, not knowing whether I was dreaming or reasoning, that I would see Virginia the next day—even if I had to go find her myself.

But when I woke up, I realized there was no way I could keep that promise. And so I stood in the doorway of my house, waiting for her to take her walk along the pier. But she never left the house.

After noon, the sky turned bright, almost serene; then the sea was a radiant turquoise.

The bathhouses cast small, oblong shadows.

Not seeing Virginia seemed like the most maddening cruelty. And in the meantime, I was convinced her husband, the lawyer Germano Secci, had taken to walking around my house with increasing frequency. If he did want to address me, as I first imagined, he might have found some way to do so. But of course, he was the one behaving as if I was supposed to acknowledge him. So I avoided him, not because I was frightened, but because there was something very sad about him. He was too tall, pale, and thin. He always wore black, and the hems of his trousers blew in the slightest breeze. He carried a large stick in his hand, and I often had the impression that his walking stick was more alive than he was. The man left me with a sense of anguish, and meanwhile my yearning for Virginia just grew more intense.

The sea glowed blue toward evening, its dark pools extending in every direction. The sailboats seemed made of gold; and there was a hint of pink in the sky at the edge of the horizon.

I remember it all well, because Virginia walked by me at that very moment. I hadn't even noticed her until she was only a few feet from me, and then I only had the time to glance up at her face. I looked around, to make sure her husband wasn't there, and then took the risk of following her. I was thinking quite seriously about talking to her this time — once evening had fallen. She went down to the pier and sat. I did the same, but I didn't sit. I stood, watching the water between the railings of the pier, hands clasped behind my back. And I listened carefully without looking at her. The wind almost made me cry. The more intense my feelings were, the more impossible it seemed to talk to her. The idea of falling into the water attracted me. The crashing of the waves seemed like chiming bells — at least to my ears.

Meanwhile the fishing boats moved out to the open water. They limped across the horizon, disappearing completely into it within the half-hour despite that snail's pace.

I took note of the fishermen sailing up close to the pier where I stood. They were looking behind me — that's how I knew Virginia was still seated there — and I blushed, so embarrassed it made my head hurt.

It was as if a bell were clanging in the midst of the frothy waves, rippling and raising the surface of the water, never stopping. Every so often the planks creaked, like a voice about to speak, and then fell silent again suddenly. I was outside of myself. What was Virginia doing? Was she thinking of me? Had she even noticed that I was there? Finally, I heard her turn away, and I wanted to do the same; but after standing still for so long, I didn't seem to know how to walk anymore. I tripped on a loose board. The distance between the sea and my house had doubled. Sometimes solitude extends space into the infinite.

The next day, while I was walking around in front of my house and smoking a cigarette, I felt a hand on my shoulder. I turned, and the lawyer Secci said to me, "You are in love with my wife."

I felt bad about lying, but I answered, "That's not true."

"Why don't you tell the truth? You're different from other men, so it shouldn't seem strange that I want to talk to you. Hear me out, and you won't be laughing then—I'm sure of it. I'm in love with my wife, too. I love her more than all of her lovers. I'm sure of that. Every year she betrays me with a new lover. No one who sees her can help but fall in love. She's beautiful. She is beauty itself. There is no other woman like her. When I want to caress her, she tells me I'm a hedonist and the only reason I love her is because I need to possess her. She taunts her lovers with those very same words. They all want her beauty—her beauty alone. We've been married five years, and in all this time, she has only become more beautiful."

Something like a shiver possessed me, but Secci persisted, clinging to my hand "Be a friend, try to share my friendship. Don't be misled by me and don't judge me as another man would. You must help me. Become her lover and take her away with you. Don't ever leave her. I want to be certain I'll never see her again. I can't ever forget her, but I'll suffer less this way. You take her."

So this man—who before had given me the impression of being underhanded or even stupid—had suddenly planted an unexpected feeling in me. And I wanted to assure him that we could be friends, so we walked in silence together by the sea.

The wind was mighty, almost thunderous. The sea roared. Lightning burst out from the blackest cloud and flashed all the way from where we stood up the coast to Rimini.

He said to me, "Let's go into your house in case she comes out. She mustn't see us together."

We went inside, but it was impossible to speak, and so we stood looking out the open window. I was troubled, and he tried to calm me with his eyes and kind expression. But I would not be calmed — after all, he had said Virginia would be coming soon.

The water became more restless, and it was getting dark. Bolts of lightning lit up the entire sea, a sudden, gloomy blue, sliced through with streaks of white foam; the sea almost glowed.

Trembling, Secci said to me, "There she is!"

I turned toward Virginia, anxiety drowning my soul. She passed by the window, supple and tall, with long legs, and breasts like those of the most sublime Grecian statue. I realized that the moment had arrived in which I must speak; yet I was terrified by voluptuous anticipation. I fell to my knees.

Secci smiled and handed me a glass of water.

(1914)

THE BOARDINGHOUSE

■ ■ ■

Two matching doors stood side by side on a landing in a dark hallway. One door led to Marta's apartment and the other to Gertrude's. People mixed them up all the time.

Marta was a widow of ten years and Gertrude was a gray-haired old maid. They had been living in that same building since they were young women, but only visited each other on religious holidays—and even then, they never actually entered each other's apartment. These were short visits that took place in the morning, right after mass and just before lunch. They lasted only long enough for the two women to discuss their health and the weather.

Marta would begin: "I bought new shoelaces."

"My girdle is stained, I'll need a new one."

"Let's hope the coming year is better."

"Let's hope."

"Good-bye. I'll let you go now."

"Let me just set down my prayerbook, and I'll come visit you."

"Then you'll see what a mess my house is."

And they would part.

After a quarter of an hour Gertrude rang Marta's doorbell. Marta, who had been waiting anxiously, would rush to open up as soon as she heard the bell.

"Won't you come in?"

"No, no. There's not much time to waste, we both have so much to do."

"You're right. So, are you feeling well?"

"I still have those aches in my knee, especially at night. And how are you?"

"I can hardly wait to die. There's not much more to say."

"Let's hope that God continues to watch over us."

"Let's hope."

"Good-bye, Signora Marta. I've spent even more time at your house than you did at mine."

"Not to worry! Not to worry. Really, it's been a pleasure."

Smiling contentedly, they did not shake hands a second time.

Their rooms had a common wall. So as soon as one woman realized she could hear what the other was doing, she would begin to move more quietly, afraid of being overheard.

Every so often, they both got out of bed or stood up from a chair at the same time, knocking against the wall in almost the same place. Then both women would freeze, waiting for the moment to pass.

In all those years as neighbors, only once, having been wakened in the night by an earthquake, did they call to each other from their beds.

"Signora Marta?"

"Signora Gertrude!"

"Were you frightened?"

"Rather!"

"Me too."

And neither wanted to utter another word. The next morning they avoided each other on the stairs.

Gertrude and Marta did nothing but think about each other. If they hadn't heard a sound from the next apartment by noon, they would go and listen at the wall.

Gertrude had a lovely cat, pure white with blue eyes that reminded her of the glass beads on her rosary. When Marta came home to find the cat waiting on the landing for Gertrude, she would quietly usher it in through her own door and feed it a piece of bread or cheese—because Marta had mice. Marta would have blushed frightfully if Gertrude were ever to find her with the cat. But that cat didn't have the slightest interest in hunting mice and cried to be let out. Finally, Marta had to open the door.

Instead of a cat, Marta had a doorbell—it didn't work as well as Gertrude's, and it took two extra hard shoves to make her door swing open. What's more, the floor in Marta's apartment shook under her feet when she walked; Gertrude's floor didn't shake. Yet both women suspected, in fact were convinced, that both apartments had the same number of rooms. And no matter how curious they both were to find out for sure, they still never asked each other.

What's more, this curiosity fostered hostility. But in an effort to be polite, they did everything they could to contain these bad feelings. Marta was slight, with sharp blue eyes; she always wore dark colors and a pale rose in her hat. Gertrude's face by contrast was smooth, and she wore an expression that was somewhere between idiotic or sinister. She was a tall woman, and her eyes could only be described as green; her hair was yellow. She wasn't a nasty person either. These two women clung to nothing from their past save a few symbols standing in for memories. Even the headstone on Marta's husband's grave was becoming gradually less visible—the stone was so eroded it could hardly be read, resting where it did under dense tufts of waxy green grass.

And when it rained, the water never managed to pass through the top leaves of the cypress trees to the headstone.

Their past had become almost entirely dissociated from their present; and they, too, had become faded as if there were no longer any strength to be drawn from the past. Any attempts at intimacy between the two women would have been in vain.

By now, the passing years were indistinguishable, and in the meantime, both women lived only for the events of each single day. The fact that the same things happened over and over again and always led to the same discussions pleased them—as if they had learned a routine by heart. Neither woman had the capacity for new thoughts—this too, due to the fact that they had matching doors.

Eventually Gertrude fell ill. She knew she was about to die; she wanted to die. She would never willingly get out of bed again. Sickness was a comfortable sensation, and she had no desire to relinquish this new-found idleness. "I am finally going to die!" she explained to everyone, as if she were talking about going on a vacation.

And then she would smile as broadly as her bed was wide, encouraging everyone else to smile along with her. Death was slow in coming, though she imagined it was only a matter of wanting it badly enough. When she thought of Marta, she would say, "She's going to live so much longer than me. How happy I am that she will live on!"

This was the closest Gertrude ever came to revenge. She played the part of a woman who finds comfort in the notion that the other person is even worse off than she is. She was always demonstrating her great fondness and sympathy for her surroundings and the people who came to visit her. She became obsessed with giving away her possessions. She could always be heard saying things like: "I leave my ring to you! What do I want with a ring after I'm dead? And you may have my silverware, as long as you promise never to sell it. But even if Marta comes to visit me, I will never never let her have my cat. She has always been so jealous of my cat!"

Soon Gertrude grew tired of watching the walls in her room, and her impatience increased daily like a fever. When death finally came, she wasn't expecting it at all.

Over the entire period of Gertrude's illness, Marta had never once come to see her! Periodically, Marta could be found out waiting on the stairs for one of Gertrude's visitors, so she could hear news about the invalid; then she would fall to her knees and beg them not to tell Gertrude that she had been asking.

Marta had stopped sleeping. It was impossible to sleep, knowing that on the other side of the wall, in a room just like her own, the oil lamp burned on through the night.

She was desperate to be more conversational about it all, to show compassion. She imagined all sorts of tender, cheerful things she could tell Gertrude. And Marta prayed. She wanted Gertrude to go to heaven.

Marta began taking care of the cat, not because she wanted it to catch mice, but because she wanted to help out Gertrude, and she wanted to become the cat's owner herself.

Then one night she dreamed that Gertrude had gotten better and was rushing swiftly over her bed without moving her legs. Where was she going? Marta tried to follow her, but she couldn't.

This dream had made her insanely jealous. Good thoughts didn't come to her anymore, and she stopped feeding the cat out of fear that maybe Gertrude wasn't going to die after all—or worse, was Gertrude planning to give her the cat as a present?

How Marta detested living under the same roof as

Gertrude—how could she have lived there so long? Why had they ever met? It made her furious to hear that doorbell ringing six, even seven times a day!

The kitchen window provided a small distraction, but she never entirely forgot Gertrude. The bells of Torre del Mangia rang every hour, cutting through the silence that pervaded Siena; and the echo, like another clock, repeated itself with peaceful clarity far into the countryside. The trees behind the hospital shaded the windows of the sick people; and the circular fountains in the garden at the foot of the wall glimmered like faded mirrors. The hills were still and sweet in the limpid air, and the cathedral was so white it hurt to look at it when the sun was shining.

Flocks of swallows endlessly filled the sky with their calls; they circled behind Marta's house, then flew so close she could almost hear the beating of their wings and almost reach out and touch them. Another flock burst from behind the Torre del Mangia; it veered to one side, then turned back. One lone swallow, scrawnier and less fluffy than the others, sat for hours and hours in the same spot. A bell would ring, and Marta could tell which church it was coming from.

She could see so many roofs from where she sat high above them; they all seemed suspended in midair. The swallows hid under the drainpipes and built nests there. A peach tree in full bloom rose above the carefully cultivated green cypress gardens. The spring air didn't stir any memories, but it made her feel better, and she derived great pleasure from knowing that Gertrude was sick and couldn't see everything she could see. Marta understood now, without understanding why, that she needed to live. She would open her window and lean out over the sill; she'd hold a bowl of scalding milk in her hands and dunk bread into it, while watching all that serenity spread out before her. She chewed slowly so she wouldn't finish her breakfast too quickly. She even went so far as to think how nice it was that her husband was dead. The feeling was inexplicable, because Marta had always loved him.

Whatever the feeling was, it made her happy. She thought, I can eat in peace, because no one is coming to take me away on a stretcher.

Despite all of this, an uncommon sadness traced back from another time clung to her, and she could see faraway things with a clarity that was almost like a painting. In certain moments, even silk flowers think they're real.

There was an ancient soul speaking through Marta, and she had no power to resist it. Her memories had artificial and independent lives. She sat watching the wall where Gertrude still lay on the other side. She stared with an air of defiance that was almost frightening—maybe because her defiance wasn't strong enough, or maybe because the walls were watching her back. She shook her fist angrily, sending a threat over to Gertrude. Why couldn't she live without thinking about Gertrude? And when they finally did come to carry her away, Marta rushed out of the house and went to sit on a bench in the public passage on the Lizza. But she wept and imagined the coffin was passing right in front of her.

So Marta launched into conversation with a nanny who was sitting on the bench next to her. This was deeply satisfying, because they talked of other matters.

And though she was ashamed of having left, she still didn't go back to the house until after nightfall.

On the stairs, in the dark, the cat brushed silently against her leg, frightening her. She let out a scream.

Marta didn't close the blinds that night so that the moonlight came into the room, and before falling asleep, she watched the walls for a long time, waiting for death's knuckles to rap her on the head.

She was climbing the stairs again two days later when, with a meow, the cat came to greet her. She rushed past the cat and into her apartment, slamming the door behind her so violently that all the rooms shook.

It didn't take much to convince her that the house wasn't right for her anymore. It was as if she had been burglarized. In fact, it seemed that everything, even the air, was wrong. She took to spending all her days outside, sitting on the first empty bench she came across in the shade of the shrubs in the public gardens. She would sit for hours watching people pass by, listening to everything, even the buzz of a fly. She stopped bringing flowers to her husband's grave in order to avoid kneeling in front of Gertrude's on her way through the cemetery. She needed to forget, to behave as if she had never met Gertrude. But instead, the dead woman seemed more alive than ever, and the two of them began holding ridiculously long conversations—so long they made Marta yawn.

At night the cat was there, getting skinnier and more disgraceful with every passing day. It was filthy, as if it had been rummaging through piles of garbage. Its body had become thin and flaccid; its nose wasn't sweet and pink anymore, but bruised and yellowish. There were bare patches on its ears. It desperately wanted to be let inside and stood crying outside Marta's door long into the night. It never shut up. That cat still belonged to Gertrude!

Finally, Marta went to the pharmacy and in a hushed voice, because she was embarrassed, begged them to sell her some poison. Marta was the kind of woman who never would have spent an extra two cents no matter what the reason, but she paid now! And she was happy. That poor creature, she thought. She wasn't going to let it die of hunger.

She trimmed the fat from the soup bone, and rather than throw it away as she usually did, she rolled it in the white powder. Then she called the cat, her heart racing with fear and pleasure. The cat jumped at the meat, chewed greedily, and swallowed it almost whole.

The garbage man found the cat's body laid out at the bottom of the stairs and tossed it into his wagon.

Marta lived another five years.

(1917)

THE TAVERN

...

We started from Florence ten days ago on a bicycle trip around the province of Emilia, and since my friend Giulio Grandi was due back at the post office for work the next morning, we left Faenza despite the pouring rain to make it back in time. It was November. The sky was gray. The streets were muddy and full of puddles. Save the occasional yellow leaf, the trees were already bare, and the fog clung to the foothills of the Apennines—all along our endless ascent.

We barely spoke. He rode ahead and I followed; or he followed and I led. Houses appeared, few and far between, and we passed them without either one of us feeling the urge to stop. We refreshed ourselves at a stand by the side of the road. Leaning the bikes up against the side, we ordered, "Two cognacs."

We drank without exchanging a word, then one of us asked, "How much?"

Giulio was off again before I finished paying.

After a few more kilometers, mud in our mouths, our eyes burning, "Are you tired?"

"A little."

"But, let's try not to slow down."

A cart passed us on the road—the driver sitting atop his load under a big green umbrella. His dog barked, and the driver let it bark as he watched us go by.

"What's this town?"

"Who cares?"

We could see people through the store windows, and the uphill climb stretched before us, and grew even steeper.

"I ache all over."

"Me too!"

"Let's sing!"

"I don't want to anymore."

"We have to sing. We have to keep our spirits up, so we don't think about being tired."

"Don't make me start calling you names."

I pushed hard against the pedals, drawing closer to him, and then up next to him.

"What's wrong? Is something bothering you?"

"A little."

I was feeling somewhat irritated myself.

I could just see his faded sweater and his hair matted under his hat, which had by now lost all its color. Every so often, I'd say something to make him turn around. His black eyes would lift just barely and then lower again, fixing on his front tire. But he'd laugh. He was a big man, with dark, hairy arms as thick as someone's leg. And I loved him like a brother. We had met at school, but I'd never—still haven't—forgotten him. He didn't talk much, at least with me, and I liked him the more for it.

I was fat, but as strong as he was, and could match him in endurance.

We stopped to eat—I can't remember where—and since they advised us to wait, because the rain was about to let up, we didn't make it any farther than Crespino that evening, only halfway between Faenza and Florence. The clouds lifted, but it didn't get any calmer outside. In the meantime, it turned cold, and dark fell early, so we ended up walking our bikes. We couldn't see twenty feet ahead, which meant that we had to stop for every noise we heard so that we wouldn't get run over. Short of calling out, which we had to do several times, it was impossible to make sure anyone knew we were there. It was black all around us, and we couldn't distinguish the mountains from the sky. As soon as we came upon the first houses of Crespino, we asked where we could eat. They answered, "There's a tavern just ahead."

Around the bend we came to an entranceway. There was a red lantern hanging outside, but the glass in it was so smoky it didn't give out any light. The curtains in the window seemed black.

I entered first. The little room was full of people moving in every direction. There was a large fireplace with a glowing fire on one side. An oil lamp hung from the ceiling, sending out more stench than light. The rumble of voices was deafening and some children — three of them, I think — were screaming.

"What are you serving for dinner?"

At first, no one even acknowledged me, and I almost had to shout my question. Then, one of the men answered me distractedly, without looking up from the polenta he was making.

"Something or other."

"Any meat?"

A woman who had a distinctly foul disposition answered this time, "Eggs . . . cold cuts . . ." And she gestured to the ham — I gathered it was ham — suspended from the ceiling.

"And bread," added someone else, as if to tell me, If you're hungry, you'll eat what's here. Don't be a bother.

I whistled to Giulio, and we pushed our bicycles inside and propped them up against a row of flour sacks. The children stopped screaming and went over to look at the bikes, touching them as if they had never seen one before. Without saying a word, the men did the same, leaning over to see better from where they sat on a bench thick as a palm tree.

Elbowing me, Giulio said under his breath, "Ask them if there is anywhere to sleep."

But the same woman from before overheard him and answered, "Yes."

She still hadn't moved and sat looking straight ahead at the wall in front of her, a colorful rag wound around her head. Her eyes were bright, and I thought, Maybe she's crazy. I could barely keep myself from staring at her. But we washed our hands and sat down. There were already plates set on the table, tiny and chipped; they looked like they might even be a little dirty. Some of the men stayed where they were, but others waved good night and left. The ones who stayed worked at the train station, or delivered coal, or were drivers.

There was an empty seat next to ours, and just to make conversation, I asked, "Who's sitting here? We could spread out more if no one's there."

One of the men, his eyes glued to me as he raised his cup to his lips, answered, "It's for the schoolteacher."

Everyone laughed and then resumed talking among themselves about other things.

Giulio remarked, "Schoolteacher? Let's hope she's attractive!"

"Let's hope," I answered with a weary smile. "Is the soup going to be ready soon?"

No one replied. But ten minutes later, the soup was emptied into our plates. That woman still hadn't moved!

"Is there something to drink? To help it go down?"

"Where's the bread?" called out Giulio, looking intently at the woman. The owner stayed where he was, on the bench by the fire with the children, who were laughing.

"Is someone going to get us bread?"

He still hadn't moved from the bench, when the school-teacher came in. She paused to say hello before she noticed us there. But no one responded; no one even looked up. Her voice gave the impression of someone talking from deep inside a cave. She blushed when she realized she would have to sit next to us, then she turned so pale it was painful. She shivered and faced the other direction.

We greeted her as politely as we knew how, trying to make her more comfortable. She was looking over at the other table, and she answered with her head bowed over her plate.

"Good evening." She finished settling in and smoothed her petticoat under her.

She laid a copy of a newsletter for teachers next to her place setting. Her name and address in red ink were visible on the mailing label, so she turned the package over.

She wasn't ugly. Her hair was fine and soft, and she didn't seem to wear it in any particular style. Her neck was long and white. She was rather thin; you could see the veins on the back of her hand through pale, unmarred skin. She had blue eyes, so sad they seemed dark; and broad, delicate eyelids. She wore a schoolgirl's smock, and she played with her bread, rolling it across the tablecloth with her fingertips, making little balls.

Giulio whispered, "Leave her alone."

"No. We should talk to her. Look at the kind of people she's surrounded by."

"Well, wait a little while."

Although the soup wasn't very good, it did us good—and not just our stomachs, either. The heaviness in our heads lifted. And I didn't want to wait anymore to talk to her. I said, "Do you teach here in the village?"

Before she answered me, she looked around, as if seeking permission from the room. Then, almost as if it were difficult to speak, she answered, "For the last three months."

She finished her soup and was pretending to wait—now that I think about it—for the second course.

"It's not very nice here, is it?"

If she had burst into tears, her voice couldn't have inspired more compassion. She lied without hesitation, "It's all right."

"Is there work here?"

"Except for seven or eight of the students, they'll all go to the mountains to be miners."

She answered our questions as if under duress, as if we were pestering her, and she couldn't understand why we cared. Why were we talking to her, anyway? I wanted to stop, so she wouldn't feel afflicted or offended. But wouldn't it be more humiliating for her if we did stop talking? Talking to us made her uncomfortable, but she liked it. Maybe, for the first time, she was able to shake off the gaze of those people who were so silent with her, so hostile. Even though, I thought, they're probably her students' parents!

Giulio, who had stopped feeling scornful, asked, "Do you come from far away?

"I'm from Faenza."

"Do your parents live there?"

"Just my mother."

Was it possible? She was giving the impression she didn't want to talk anymore—employing that unpleasant, passive malevolence women learn. I imagined her as a schoolgirl: gracious and hardworking, a little coarse, and a little too clever.

She started eating, taking each bite as if she were worried that they were talking about her or making fun of her.

So we kept quiet.

A train passed over the bridge; almost directly over our heads. The whole room shook. Then, silence fell again.

"Is it still raining?" I asked the owner. He opened the door and said, facing the railway workers rather than me, "It's about to snow."

"Snow?"

"It's going to snow through the night."

I punched Giulio's shoulder and teased, "It's going to be iced over tomorrow morning!"

The schoolteacher pulled the newsletter from its wrapper and started reading. I could see her name on the mailing label.

I told my friend, "Her name's Assunta."

He laughed. Then I asked, "Is that a journal of teaching methods?"

She looked at it, turning it over in her hands, as if she were seeing it for the first time, and answered, "Yes, sir."

"Do you read books, too?"

She smiled, "Some. I brought them from Faenza."

"Novels?"

"Yes, sir."

Her voice was a murmur, and she went back to reading until they put a plate with a slice of Parmesan cheese down in front of her. She started eating. I noticed drops of blood from her teeth staining the bread. I told Giulio, "She won't tell me what she reads."

"What do you care?"

I was getting angry with him, but I asked, "What should I talk to her about?"

"Leave her alone."

She was ready to leave, but she seemed embarrassed about getting up so quickly. I asked the woman who still hadn't moved, "Are the beds warmed?"

"They should be, soon."

I asked under my breath, "Who is she?"

"She's the owner. She's blind. They'll give her something to eat now."

And then, her husband did put a pot of soup on her lap and handed her a steel spoon that she wrapped her lips around and sucked with every mouthful.

With amusement, one of the railway workers decided to let us know what everybody had been thinking since we first entered, "Aren't you *tired*."

Inasmuch as I understood what he meant, I answered, "Yes, and we're sleepy, too."

"I'll buy that!"

And he turned back toward his companions, continuing with a sly laugh, "You'd have to be crazy to go out in this weather!"

They all burst out laughing for the second time, their insolence so brutal it was almost innocent.

Then Giulio called out, "What's it to you?"

No one answered. They just stared at us. One of them was still laughing, his head bowed low.

"Can you bring us some cigarettes?"

"What kind?" asked the owner more politely than before—as if he were doing us a favor, or else putting the others in their place.

But when someone rubbed Giulio the wrong way he didn't get over it quickly. Instead, he'd become agitated with me, or with whoever crossed his path. He answered, "Whatever fine gentlemen smoke."

The schoolteacher shifted toward him. She didn't look at him, but there was a hint of a smile on her face.

The owner, moving more quickly now, brought us the cigarettes.

The shop in the tavern sold anything that you could need in such a small town, and it was the only one there was. The schoolteacher shifted, trembled, maybe. We began to smoke and offered her one, too. This time, before she answered, she dared look at us. Her gaze was so shy yet so determined that it would have made it impossible to lie to her or be rude. It was, nonetheless, one of those transparent gazes that didn't reveal anything. She answered, "I don't smoke."

We were truly ashamed. There was something in her voice that conveyed an allusion to those men, but we didn't know whether it was anger or resignation. The way she tilted her head, it almost seemed that she liked the smell of smoke, that it made her head spin a little. But she remained calm; she wasn't going to give anything away.

When she turned to look at us again—I don't know why, maybe Giulio had rattled his plate with his fist—her eyes were more serene, more intense, rapt in a dream. A suggestion of a smile passed over her lips, but died before it appeared. There was a soft down on her upper lip; it glowed white against the light. I began to have that sense of well-being, of calm, almost confidence—the feeling you get when you are sitting next to a woman who is even just a little pretty, and there are no double meanings, and feelings are dreamed about.

She knotted her napkin and pushed it through a metal ring with a braid of her initials etched into it. I noticed that her polished fingernails seemed too heavy for her fingers. Not having any pretext to stay longer, she rose and barely nodded in our direction, as if she wanted to erase the conversation we'd just had.

The blind woman's breathing was restless.

Within half an hour, we'd smoked the whole pack of cig-arettes and the workers had left. We headed off to our room, too. Giulio said, "You should really be born in a place like this to work as a teacher here. They shouldn't send them so far away from home. It's the same everywhere. How can you expect someone to live here? Why ask someone to make such a sacrifice, especially when she's so different from everyone else? All they know how to do around here is make babies!"

"You're right. But, we're only thinking about it because we're here . . . Tomorrow, once we're back in Florence, we won't even remember it."

Our room was dim and low; there was a rosette molding laced with vines in the middle of the ceiling.

Once we'd turned off the lamp, we noticed a streak of light from the room next to ours; there was someone there.

We got up quietly, and slowly, holding our breath, we went into the hallway.

It was the schoolteacher's room.

Through the crack in the door, we saw her turning the pages of a book she wasn't reading, and crying. Then she began to get undressed, reaching behind her neck for the but-tons.

(1914)

HOUSE FOR SALE

. . .

I knew the three men had come to see me about my house, which was for sale, but I was still pleased to overhear them asking for me. From my room, I could hear that the maid didn't want to let them in. She tried to tell them I wasn't home, but I flung open my door and came out. My voice trembled when I greeted them, then my body followed suit. They laughed as they answered me, winking to each other, and making a joke out of my foolishness. They probably thought I didn't notice. They didn't seem to care one way or another, anyway. I knew very well what was going on, but didn't intend to let it dampen my spirits. I jumped right in, wringing my hands, "Have you come to see the house? You'll be glad you came."

First, I led them through my apartment, which was the smallest in the house. They examined everything. They even paused in front of a loose brick. The one with the cane, Signor Achille, tapped the walls, trying to determine how thick they were. They picked up objects off the tops of the furniture, they felt the curtains. One of the other gentlemen, Signor Leandro, leaned out the window to spit. Then we moved on to the other apartments, where my boarders lived. The boarders welcomed me with hostility and amazement.

But since I was happy to pretend I wasn't listening, they began to say nasty things about me to the three buyers. Plans were already being made for when they would take over as landlords. No one showed me any respect. I walked at the rear of the group. They all stood and talked as long as they pleased, while I looked at the walls of my house, maybe for the last time ever. Then I stopped looking at the walls. I went in and out of rooms as if I didn't know what I was doing or why I was even there.

When we returned to my apartment, the third gentleman let me know his nickname was Piombo—for lead. He said, "We have already wasted too much time. What are you asking, Signor Torquato?"

I wanted to distance myself from the entire affair. I didn't even want to consult someone else. I could have asked ten thousand, but I said eight thousand. I was worried even that would be too much and the men would leave without making a counter offer.

Signor Achille chided me severely. "Which one of us do you want to sell to? There are three of us here."

I answered, "I thought you were all buying it; the three of you together."

Piombo answered, "I wouldn't even give you three thousand for it."

I was confused and risked commenting, "That wouldn't be enough to cover the mortgage, which is seven thousand. I was asking for eight thousand, so that I would have at least one thousand left over—for myself." Smiling, I turned red.

"And what would you do with a thousand lire?"

"I . . . I don't have anything else. I could live a few months on that."

"One month more or less, what does it matter?"

"That's true," I answered.

"But you can't make a deal with all three of us at the same time."

"I agree."

"So, you should keep quiet."

Then Signor Leandro proposed, "I'll give you seven thousand. That will take care of the mortgage."

"And for me?"

"That's not my problem."

I felt very sympathetic toward Signor Leandro. Meanwhile, the other two men were putting on a show of being upset that I had figured out there was only one real buyer among them. The other two had come along to pretend they were interested in buying the house, to offer less, and bring the price down. I understood perfectly well, but I didn't mind. Actually, I was offended that they thought they needed to resort to such tactics—as if I weren't an honest man, as if I would try to get more money than I needed to pay off the mortgage. I didn't want anything anyway. I wanted to be left with nothing.

Signor Leandro, the real buyer, was a merchant, though I don't know what he sold—maybe grain. He had a red face and a black mustache. Signor Achille was blond, and Piombo was old with gray hair. While we were busy having this discussion, I told Tecla, the maid, to make us some coffee. They couldn't have cared less. The real buyer said impatiently, "Enough chatter! Let's get this over with. Do you accept or not? We don't need to drink your coffee, we can afford to buy coffee for ourselves elsewhere."

I answered, "I only asked her to make coffee because I was trying to be friendly. I wanted to make you feel welcome."

"Who cares!"

The old man said, "Rather than making coffee, you could

give me the chance to make an offer. I wouldn't give you more than six thousand for this house."

The blond man shook his head, as if he pitied the other two men for their stupidity in offering me all that money. It seemed I had set them against each other. This made me feel so embarrassed and humiliated that I wanted to just give them the house; but there was still the mortgage to think of. Now I was ashamed of my mortgage, because it didn't leave me free to act as I would have liked to under the circumstances.

Signor Leandro continued, "If you are satisfied with my first offer, even though I already regret it, we can draw up the contract today at my lawyer's office."

How could I have possibly refused? Hoping he hadn't noticed how fragile I was feeling, I proposed, "I can come before lunch, if that would be better for you."

But he was offended. "I have other, much more important things than this to take care of!"

In order to keep him from speaking so rudely to me, I said, "Forgive me. I had no idea."

"Let's stop the small talk, okay? Two o'clock, no later, I'll meet you at my lawyer's office."

Then I was embarrassed I didn't know who his lawyer was, but I dared to ask him anyway. He told me his lawyer was Signor Bianchi, Esquire—"Do you know where his office is?"

"If I could just have his address—I wouldn't want to get lost."

In the meantime, Tecla had brought the coffee. But it had absolutely no flavor and was burnt, so I was at a complete loss for words and very concerned they would notice how awful it was.

Signor Achille, the blond man said, "Now that you have forced your coffee on us, don't you think we should discuss the brokerage fee for me and him?" He indicated Piombo with his cane.

As if just beginning to wake up, I answered, "The brokerage fee?"

"Of course! Do you think we came along for the fresh air?"

"But I don't have a cent!"

Now I didn't know if they were ever going to forgive me. Indeed, Signor Achille raised his cane as though he were going to crack me over the head.

"You think so little of us?" He grabbed my arm. I wanted to tell them they should get the fee from the buyer, but I was too worried about how Piombo might react. I looked around and, pale with emotion, I said, "If you please, I could give you this wardrobe . . ."

"Is that all you have?"

I responded quickly, hoping to make everything seem friendlier, "There's my bed over there. And the copper pans in the kitchen."

"Are they still good?"

"It's all still good," and I asked the maid to bring some pans in to show them.

"I thought we were going to do serious business here!" said the old man Piombo with a look of indulgence.

That made my heart ache. But I didn't have anything else to give them. I even scanned the ceiling for something, but there was really nothing left at all.

They drank the coffee and finished the sugar, eating whole chunks of it at a time. I preferred not to fill my cup, hoping they would realize I had made the coffee especially for them. I really wanted them to know that. But they didn't so much as thank me. Piombo suggested, "Why don't you add these cups to the brokerage fee, Signor Torquato?" At that,

Signor Achille landed a blow on his neck. "And which one of us should he give them to?"

In order to calm Signor Achille down, I said, "I don't use those cups anymore."

The buyer picked his nose. He was already absorbed making plans for the house. To that end, he asked me, "When can the rooms be vacated?"

I had been thinking about staying on for another few days, but since he asked so directly, I answered, "I can be out today, as soon as we've drawn up the contract."

"Good. Good!"

"I'm sorry I can't leave sooner."

"It is a shame."

At that point, I began to feel as if my heart were being wrenched from my body. And he seemed to notice my mood immediately; he asked in a threatening voice, "You haven't changed your mind, have you?"

I responded with some effort, "No. No! Quite the opposite! I was thinking of something else."

"That's all we need now, is for you to have second thoughts! We're all adults here, not children! You probably haven't thought about the fact that these two men here witnessed our agreement."

"I assure you," I said, "I was thinking about something else!"

"God willing, you seem to have your wits about you." He walked over to a wall and said, "Tomorrow, I'm sending someone over to clean up all these rooms and reinforce the crossbeams. I'm going to have him check the roof, too, because the boarders on the top floor told me there's a drip when it rains."

"Yes, it's true, there's a broken tile. I haven't fixed it yet, because I haven't had the money."

"Then I'm going to have him redo the façade and paint the shutters. The whole thing is going to cost me another thousand. Doesn't that seem like a lot of money to you?"

I was impressed by all the work he was planning and offered, "Then you'll see what a beautiful house this can be!"

"Did you think we were going to let it go to ruin the way you did?"

The way he talked to me was thoughtless. His tone suggested I had done something wrong. I was left without any way of answering him. No matter how hard I concentrated, I couldn't seem to come up with the words that would express my feelings. All I wanted to do was to stop him from talking to me like that. But he was blaming everything on me, and I was hurt. I couldn't think straight, so I said, "I'll leave my family pictures on the walls, I don't know where else to put them . . ."

"You can throw them out."

"Are they in your way?"

"Didn't I just get finished telling you I'm going clean this place up!"

Then he took Signor Achille's cane and knocked down almost the entire row of pictures, the ones without frames. I would have liked to pick them up, but decided to wait until after they had left. I really did want them to know that those pictures were of my mother and sister, who were both dead now. Maybe then they would understand how I felt. But I didn't dare say anything. Signor Leandro was the new landlord, and he had knocked it all down. I didn't want to do anything that might upset them. There was a photograph of my father still hanging on the wall above where the others had been, so I said, "Knock that one down, too!"

But he wasn't interested in such nonsense and shrugged his shoulders. What he did, instead, was to grab hold of an old flower vase I'd been keeping. It was another memento of my sister. When he realized that the dust on the vase had dirtied his fingers, he said, "I shouldn't have touched that."

"Would you like to wash up?" I offered.

Signor Leandro decided to use his handkerchief instead, although soiling it appeared to anger him greatly. I had become terrified that something else would happen as a result of his curiosity. So I suggested, "We can go down now if you like."

But one of the others asked, "Do you know if your maid steals things? Keep in mind that she's responsible for this stuff, and it's all ours now."

My hand over my heart, I answered, "I swear that not a crumb will be missing!"

"Well, just to be sure, it would be better if you gave us the keys now. That way the maid can leave with us, and we'll lock up."

"As you distrust me, we'll do as you say. Tecla, come! We're all leaving together."

The maid, who was an old widow, said, "And when will I get the chance to gather my things?"

The buyer answered, "I'll let you in, if you come back tonight."

"But what about my pay for this past month?"

The three of them burst out laughing. I was so embarrassed I didn't know what to say.

"We'll talk about it outside."

Signor Achille said, "Wouldn't that be something if you couldn't sell your house because of a maid!"

I told him, "She doesn't understand anything. She is not well educated. But she'll leave with me. I'll make sure she obeys."

The five of us all left together. Tecla was the last one out, and she closed the door.

The only thing I could do then was go to lunch. At two o'clock sharp, I was at the lawyer's. Actually, I was the first to arrive. I signed the deed, which had been written on official paper, and I wrote my name as beautifully as I knew how, even though my hand was trembling. I tried to figure out if they were happy with me and whether I might have said something to contradict the impression I would have liked them to have of me. I waited to see if they wanted anything else. But the lawyer said, "You're all set!"

And he put a red stamp on the contract.

Signor Leandro dismissed me, saying, "You can leave now, Signor Torquato."

I said good-bye, as I always do, with respect. Nobody answered. They were already talking among themselves by the time I reached the door.

I went down the stairs from the lawyer's office, walking as if a weight had been lifted off me. I don't remember what I did next or how I spent the rest of the day. By evening I had nothing to eat and nowhere to sleep. I was exhausted, but did everything I could to be strong. It started pouring rain as night fell. So I went to find shelter under the drainpipes of my house that was now sold. I was so sad. I wanted to be happy, or at least as happy as I had been that morning, for I knew my boarders would be eating supper at this hour, and the people down in the neighborhood usually played the piano. Those neighbors were always playing some new polka.

(1918)

THE CRUCIFIX

■ ■ ■

I thought: a world of God's creation is left unfinished. Its matter is not alive, not dead. The vegetation is all identical in this world, and the rough sketches of formless beasts are unable to move out from their muck because they have neither legs nor eyes.

The plants in this world cannot be distinguished by their color—because they have none. This world would also have its own odor—but only when spring is approaching; and so it's a rather muddy smell. Adam is there, too—a rough version of him—he has no spirit, no soul. He cannot talk or see, but he feels the mire around him moving, and it frightens him.

There is neither a sun nor a moon. This world lies in the loneliest corner of infinity, where there are no stars, where a lone comet goes to die, as if in exile. This half-life is more ancient than our own.

These are, nonetheless, landscapes of profound beauty; landscapes that harbor what beauty there is in our souls and in the souls of each delicate creature of our world.

Twilight is continuous there, so the mire—almost red in that light—gleams like gold. And even we can recognize the color of the sea in the wet clay stretching along the water.

But Adam, trapped in his half-formed state, blind as he is,

thinks the opaqueness that surrounds him is light. And when the storm winds blow over his skin, he believes he is walking.

If touched, the leaves on the plants would fall to pieces and their crumbs turn to paste in our hands. A strong rain destroys entire forests, which grow again — once the air turns warm — like the mushrooms of our own world.

But it would be difficult to distinguish a river from a sea; where there is a lake today, there is a mountain tomorrow. And beyond, the plains are almost red and extend to the horizon, the turbulent horizon. Or else, a shy, muddy blue, aglow in the morning and blackened by night, can be seen just over the boulders and rocks by the water.

But it's a blacker river than any other that slices through the vast plain; so black it can be seen from far away, even at night. And in the wake of this river is born not poplar trees, but a foliage so thick and dense it is impossible to penetrate. Summer is all black, formed of hot shadows instead of sun. Storms are muffled by fog and clouds, so much so that they are almost silent when they pass over the river.

And even in the thickest hour of darkness, the river is completely visible.

Such were my thoughts one Sunday afternoon while sitting on the banks of the most dirty and lonesome point of the Tiber. I was staring at a row of houses that seemed to have been split into halves when they put down those two or three new roads. I could see right into the filthy rooms — colors faded and dripping down the outer walls, tufts of grass sprouted from holes crammed with mortar. It was grass that makes no blossom, shiny grass, horrifying grass, grass no animal would eat.

And why was I thinking such thoughts? There was a girl standing near me. I hadn't seen her arrive. She was barefoot. Her thin, black hair was pulled back on her head by a single

clip. Her hair was most like a disgusting cobweb. Her forehead was greasy and covered with puckered boils. Her dress
was faded and old. It didn't fit her well, and she had to hold
it down on her hips with her hands. She looked as though
some kind of slop bucket brimming with filth had been
dumped over her, leaving stains on her skin. Her face was
rather round and babyish. Her mouth was large, and its
shape almost identical to one of the boils on her forehead or
neck — around which she wore a soiled string. Her eyes were
round too, and their color, at that moment, was undeniable —
though they were completely lacking any character, human
or animal. There seemed to be something behind her eyes
blocking anything from getting through.

At that hour, there was really no one in that spot on the
banks of the Tiber. The bark on the plane trees was stripped,
ugly. The dead part of Rome, extending down the river from
where we stood, seemed so distant, as though we had somehow left the city behind us.

I didn't want to speak. I felt that in order to speak to that
young girl I would have to completely forget not only my
conscience, but everything else in my memory too.
Otherwise, it would be impossible. I, too, could sense myself
abolishing life and my inner self, and so becoming identical to
the creature standing before me. I was almost frightened. I
don't believe I'd have suffered a more empty and arid sense
of solitude had I been standing in the middle of a desert.

Yet, in the silence, I drew an odd and sudden lucidity
from the sun. I could see the dome of San Pietro, and it meant
nothing to me! All of it seemed unformed. And there was no
possibility of imagining it in some other way; the cathedral
was gloomy, like the houses cleaved open before me.

The girl was the child of an unmarried woman. As a baby,
she slept behind the public toilets. By the age of twelve or

thirteen, maybe earlier, she had lost her virginity. Her mother went off somewhere and left her alone. One Sunday night, her drunk mother just didn't come back from the tavern. Almost everyone gave food to the girl, as they would to a stray dog. Whoever wanted her took her. They would give her half a liter of wine and a plate of macaroni in payment. All she has is her dress and a jumper. She wears stockings and colored slippers in the winter. Whoever wants her, comes to her, smiles, and then leads her away. She tells them her name, but she's the only one who remembers it—and people always rename her anyway.

For a while, after they first knocked down the shacks, she would sleep in the rubble, next to the dog the foreman left there on a chain at night so that no one would steal the doors, beams, scrap iron, and all the other salvageable remnants of an old house. In the dark, someone sees her, wakes her, and then leaves her where he found her. She spends her days sleeping because she is always tired.

At night, she washes as best she can at the fountain. She even cleans her legs and everything else at the fountain. In the meantime, she is wishing, but not too hard, that they will let her sleep in one of the wooden barracks covered with left-over, rusted tinplate, which sit on the gravely shores of the Tiber, between the Ponte del Risorgimento and the Ponte Milvio.

Many soldiers come by here at the end of the day. If there are two or three of them, they beat her. But she doesn't let herself cry, because they're having fun. She tries to enjoy herself, too. Then she follows them until they shoo her away, threatening to cut her if she doesn't leave. She watches them walk off, sad about having been left alone. And when her shoulders or arms ache from the beating, she pinches her flesh hard—but still doesn't cry. She won't look anyone in the face unless she's forced to—in that way, she thinks she is doing them a favor. If someone asks for a kiss, she won't do it, worrying the man will think she's disgusting afterward. She is so modest that she doesn't want to look. It hurts her to think that even for a moment someone likes her, but she won't let it show, because whenever she does, she gets pushed away with a slap on the mouth or a wrench of the neck. That makes her blush in shame.

By now, she craves their attention, if only to be sure that someone can like her. And she is sad, her feelings hurt, on the days no one comes by for her.

She is so close to me—waiting for me to take her in my arms. But, as if frightened by my own thoughts, I leave.

One Sunday, I walk from the Coliseum to the Roman Forum. Behind a church wall, there is a pile of scraps and garbage. Blades of grass like long, straight, green needles have grown through the wall from the inside out.

She sleeps there, on top of the pile. She is curled up in her dress, pale—from weariness, I'm sure. Flies circle her head; their wings are iridescent like her hair.

The sun is so bright it hurts my head. Here and there the grass glimmers and gleams. It had rained several hours earlier; the earth is still steaming.

The girl's dress is soaked, although the spikes of wood in the iron gate are already dry. And the sun's luster spreads over the stones of the ruins. The footpaths are pools of water. But the trees on the Palatino are sweet, and the roses dripping with water smell like they do when you take them in your hands and crush them. The marble is resplendent and sharp as glass at the broken edges.

The lizards seem like green stones—but alive. The sky over the Coliseum is almost gemlike.

If she wakes up, I have decided to speak to her this time.

True, I'm still embarrassed, of course I am, because who knows what people will think if they see me.

And because there are moments in which, whistling an unrecognizable tune, you think you have made poetry and all your thoughts seem to have miraculous beauty, I cannot think about the girl any longer. I avert my eyes quickly, almost instinctively, from her image. Standing where I am, I forget about her gradually, completely.

The light dies, and dust rises around the Coliseum, almost to the top, and seems to hover there, uplifted. A hill with a convent at top hides behind the trees—it has its own cypresses. A Forum caretaker comes out of his painted wooden hut. Holding his watch in his hand, he takes a step and then stops. Two crows lift off from the top of the church, making it look like the roofs themselves are spinning. The earth finishes drying out, washed, all clean now, become as pure as the air.

I love her, then, the earth. And it seems that if I were to speak, my voice would possess her sweetness. I understand why the sun illuminates her and why the trees are so beautiful with their leaves. Then, I look at the hedges and the flowers near and far.

Yet, by the church wall, the heat burns over the wooden crucifix, as if wanting to pull the nails from His feet and wrists. And the young girl awakens, as if rising from that pile of waste.

(1918–19)

POVERTY

■ ■ ■

Lorenzo Fondi was looking at his wife's hat on the bureau. It was ugly, the ribbons were faded, but he wanted to kiss it. Outside, the air was glowing as if it were about to burst into flames; and inside the bedroom, it was so bright you almost had to shade your eyes. By the window stood a dusty table and a pile of books, never opened anymore; books bought so many years before—right out of school—now littered with flyspecks. A pair of filthy, tattered gloves that hadn't been worn since last winter lay next to the books. The clothing on the rack was old.

But he wasn't in love with his wife anymore, and he wanted to leave. He'd pawned a couple of cows and was thinking about skipping the country with the money. He was bored with his life as a small landowner; a life of bills, taxes, and end of the year accounts! His workers stole from him as much as they could get away with, and profits were bad. He'd never thought about what else he might do in order to lead a more peaceful life—but there must be something better out there! His father had been a good farmer and had even put together some savings.

He was full of rage as he fastened his collar and glanced over his new jacket, the one he'd been so anxious about buying

Suddenly, still watching himself in the mirror, he stopped to listen. The workers were starting to thresh the grain. He had to escape soon! On the evening train. He had to; it was imperative! He looked at himself again and laced his shoes. He was about to change them for a less worn-out pair, when Corrada, his wife, came in. He became even more anxious.

"Did you collect the money for that wine from Signora Viola?"

He answered at the top of his lungs, "I told you I didn't!"

"Well, when are you going to? We owe the butcher. It's been over a month."

His lips tightened with anger. He yelled again, "It'll get paid in time!"

"But I'm embarrassed."

Two, even three tears dropped down the woman's cheeks.

"Whenever I pass by the store, he watches me as if he wanted to ask me when I'm going to pay."

Corrada was having difficulty speaking. Her mouth was twisted horribly with pain.

"That's just your stupid imagination! The butcher, and everybody else, thinks we're rich."

He quickly added, almost under his breath, "That's why he trusts us, because he really thinks we're wealthy. Don't worry about it!"

Corrada stopped crying and clasped her hands together.

"Where are you going, all dressed up like that?"

"To Siena. I'm going to see that guy who bought hay from us last year."

His wife, the daughter of a civil servant, was pale and slight, her eyes set into ashen, almost transparent, skin. With a sigh, she put her hands on his shoulder and said, "You don't like to talk about money; but what are we going to do?"

He shrugged her hands away. Then he said with a laugh, "I don't want to talk about it."

And Corrada grew even paler. "You always say that. You're cruel."

"What do you want me to say? There's no other kind of answer. Even if it were all up to me."

She stopped talking and wrung her hands. He looked back at her almost resentfully and could feel himself turning red with shame. It was insufferable to be standing there like this in front of her, as if he were a guilty man. Because deep down, though he didn't understand to what extent, misfortune was twisting his soul.

She went to the window and pressed her face against the glass. She didn't turn around while her husband finished getting dressed. When he opened the bedroom door, he said, "Where are you going?"

"To Manderò, tomorrow morning, to sell chickens."

Just to make conversation, Lorenzo said, "Oh, so you have to sell some chickens?"

"Yes! We'd starve to death if it weren't for me. And I have to pay back Vittoria for the anchovies."

"Keep your voice down, the workers will hear us."

"I know. I know. You don't have to tell me. You're the only one who's allowed to shout. Everyone else has to keep quiet."

"I shout, but not about money."

And he stomped at the ground.

She blushed again, on the verge of tears, wiped her eyes and ran from the room.

"So! Now *you've* left!"

But in the end, why blame her? He understood that he'd been wrong to think he'd ever loved her—loved her passionately and beyond reason. But why didn't she understand that? Why couldn't she see, too? Why wasn't she smiling instead of crying?

Meantime, he was no longer sure he should leave forever! He sat down, a cold sweat on his forehead, as if he were nauseous and about to vomit. His anxiety over the payments and debts was indescribable. His soul felt turned inside out. How often would he have preferred to fall to the ground dead than take out another loan? Healthy and strong, just twenty-seven years old, and dead on the ground!

Corrada was sitting and darning a pair of old socks. Little by little, she stopped crying—though the tears left stains on her apron. She wasn't mad at her husband. She was even a little sorry she'd spoken to him like that! And she became distracted by thoughts of chickens and pigeons.

More than anything, he couldn't stand knowing that she was so unhappy! Whenever he saw her washing plates or doing the laundry, he'd leave rather than watch her. Though it never occurred to him to help her.

In the meantime, Corrada was beginning to feel a little better. She felt almost reassured by the excitement. And thinking about how much she loved her house gave her a most pleasant sensation.

So why wasn't business going better? Why shouldn't it be? She'd have to fix that. She tucked the socks away into the overflowing yarn basket. She got to her feet, wiped a handkerchief across her face, and stood stiffly by the window.

When she heard her husband moving around again, she returned to the bedroom.

"How much will you get for the hay?"

"I don't know."

"Why don't you know?"

"I don't know what the prices are this year."

"Make sure you find out before you go making deals."

Although the topic was business, her voice was tender, almost affectionate. He looked at her and hid his anger. Moments before he'd considered wringing her neck. But he agreed with her now. And now, he couldn't leave anymore; he couldn't say a word to her. Just then, there was a knock at the door.

"Who's there?" she asked.

He felt that distress again; it was like being suffocated.

"It's me."

It was his little second cousin.

Corrada motioned that she should enter. But Lorenzo stopped her. "What do you want?" he asked with no kindness in his voice.

"I have a letter here."

Corrada took it. The little girl added, "They're waiting for an answer."

And she left. Corrada opened the envelope and went white, like a rag in bleach. He didn't want to watch her fingers tremble.

"It's the bill from the carpenter."

"How many times has he sent it?"

"This is the fourth time already."

"Tell him I'll pay it as soon as we sell the grain. They're threshing it today. We can sell it in a week."

"What about everything else? When will all that be taken care of? Look at how I'm dressed!"

He turned red and bit down on his bottom lip for a long time. Then his wife wanted to give him a hug. He put his hands on her chest and pushed her away.

"Go tell him what I just said."

She started crying again.

"How come you don't go? I have to do everything that you don't like to."

He yelled, "There's nothing I don't like to do!"

Red with anger, he added, "I have to dust my hat right now. Tell him to wait. Why are you crying? There's nothing to cry about. You're just going to make me angrier. I've had enough."

She fled, slamming the door. Lorenzo swung it open again after her. He cursed and bellowed: "Why can't you just die!"

Cesira, his stepmother, was coming out of her room. She told him, "Why are you like that?"

"What concern is it of yours? You don't pay my bills, do you?"

She grew pale and then blushed. "Everything has its time."

She was about forty years old and short, and her face was always red—a real peasant.

He crumpled his hat and spit at the books. He bumped into the table and then shoved it against the wall. All the books fell.

He located something akin to delight in the depths of his rage. This house! This house! If only a bolt of lightening would come down and split it in two, kill his wife, his stepmother, his little cousin. Just take it all! His heart pounded like the peasants working the thresher—even harder perhaps. He went to the drawer and pulled out the thousand lire borrowed against the cows, the whole wad of it. He stopped to listen.

His wife was yelling at his stepmother. Her voice was raw, but sounded more pained than if she'd been crying. He listened further. How long was that going to go on? He must stop her. And he couldn't talk to his stepmother about anything.

He realized they weren't blaming him; but they were going on about business, and they seemed to agree with each other. He thought ironically, *Yes. You two gang up. That'll solve everything.*

His stepmother said, "We've got to find some kind of solution. We're headed for disaster!"

"What can we do? I defy you to come up with a solution."

"Think of it however you want."

"I'm going to suggest that we take out a mortgage."

"Won't that make things worse?"

"What should we do instead?"

"Go to a lawyer for advice."

"Right away. I'll get dressed and go into the city."

His stepmother added something in a low voice. Then the door opened. Corrada entered, already half undressed to change her clothes. She said, "I'm coming with you."

"What for?"

"It's none of your concern."

"I know what you're up to. And that other fool's been encouraging you."

"That's just fine! I have as much right as you do to think about our life. Go give the carpenter his answer."

He snorted and headed down the stairs.

The boy who had brought the bill was leaning on his bicycle, waiting.

"Tell the carpenter that I'll come by in a few days."

The boy straightened up, waved soberly, and left. The grain in the barn reflected the sun. One of the less timid chickens came over, stretching its neck as long as was possible, snapped up a seed and sped off to eat in safety. It flapped its wings.

Cesira opened the window and called, "Lorenzo!"

"What do you want?"

"Come up."

He shrugged his shoulders. He didn't want to leave anymore. Instead, he was thinking with the confidence of a landowner that he would be able to pay off the cows on time.

Maria was walking by. She was the daughter of one of the peasants. She smiled as she passed him. She wasn't wearing a corset, and her large breasts fascinated him. She went into the house, where she had been kneading dough. She was covered with flour. Cautiously, he drew toward the open door, growing pale with the desire to fall into her arms. Her smile called to him, a sensual smile that bound him to her. He would surely be able to speak to her later in the evening by the shed: *I'm going away again next year. Business is getting better!*

He walked up the stairs, leaning down to stroke the cat that was sidling along the stairway.

His stepmother said, "Why do you treat your wife so badly?"

"What did I do? I got mad."

"Go find her."

He opened the bedroom door, full of good will, and asked, "So have you really decided to come to Siena?"

"You got it. I'm not like you are — you can't make decisions."

And, as she had finished dressing, she pulled on her hat and grabbed her umbrella.

"Am I going alone?"

"Yes. I'm going to stay here to watch over the workers."

She agreed, happy at last.

(1917–18)

DEAD MAN IN THE OVEN

...

Cecco drank not just to feel happy, but also, as he put it, to warm his blood—especially in the winter when he woke three hours before daybreak in order to water his two mules and harness them to the cart he used to transport bricks from the ovens to wherever they were building a new house. He'd get drunk sometimes for two days running. Then, you could hear him singing from a mile away.

The farmers always recognized him as he came up the road and would laugh and wave. If he'd fallen asleep in his cart, they would throw clumps of dirt at him instead. He was already an old man. Thin. His beard was white. He was always covered with limestone and brick dust. His shoes were worn out and unlaced. His socks had been darned everywhere. The mules were old, too, and could barely stand by themselves. Half skinned from the abuse and beatings of former masters, their knees were swollen, and their harnesses had more twine to them than leather. Their bells had long stopped ringing. Their bits were coming undone. The cart was in pieces; the wheels were uneven, rusty iron wire bound the wooden planks together. It listed heavily to one side. The boards were so soft and warped that more often than not the cart would just break down in the middle of the road. Then

Cecco would get an old door from someone, which he placed over the bottom of the cart and, as best as he could, load up again. He didn't give the mules much to eat—although he often claimed that if he were a richer man, he'd have gotten his mules drunk, too! As he neared home, he let them loose to graze with the sheep in an abandoned meadow where the grass never had a chance to sprout.

Finally, the cart collapsed, and Cecco sold the pieces for firewood. The two mules were released into the meadow. One drowned, having wandered too far into the Tressa River. A miller stole the other one, and it gave out under the weight of two bags of grain while climbing a hill. At first, Cecco had nowhere to go, so he slept in the stall. But then another brick-carter rented the stall and sent Cecco away. So he found an oven behind a peasant's house near Coroncina, close to a tavern. Every night, he'd wriggle his way into the oven and hide. No one knew how exactly, but he always found some way of getting drunk, and he would sing as he made his way back to the oven. For months at a time, Cecco sang instead of talking.

He didn't even respond to the women who would call him from their doorways. He'd accept a piece of bread or a few pennies and show his gratitude by making a silly face. The priest at Pecorile gave him plates of meat, but would lecture him, too. Cecco lowered his head, clasped his scrawny, hairy hands together, and sang something happy—even though his voice had acquired a distinct tremble.

"If only I had become a priest, like you!"

"They would have taken your parish away in no time."

Cecco put his hand to his head and answered, "Oh, it's true. It's so true.

> "When you whirl you make a wheel
> So whirl and whirl and whirl and whirl!"

After talking to the priest, he would say to the first woman who happened by, "I don't believe in the Church. I don't believe in the saints. I can't bring myself to believe any of it. Is that my fault? I'm not this way on purpose. It's just that I'd rather have a glass of wine . . . Rather have a glass of wine without water added to it."

And then he'd end up groping the women — in good fun. They'd step back and pretend to call for their husbands so that he would go away.

Cecco always went happily — turning around to stick his tongue out and sneer. That made the women laugh. He walked miles and miles, from morning to night, until he couldn't walk anymore. The workers who remembered him from his days carting bricks would give him some money or old clothes, which he would sell to the next person he met along the way. Sometimes, when he was alone, he stopped right in the middle of the road, made a fist, and stared longingly — looking at it as if it were a glass. He'd bring it to his lips. He walked a few more steps and stopped again and then repeated the gesture.

When it was time for the *vendemmia* and he saw the grapevines — rows of them running down the hillsides and flush up to the hedges at the end of the fields, as if they wanted to climb out onto the road — Cecco would look forward to the harvest and feel vigorous and young again. He walked taller. Sometimes, when he was alone, he would stop in front of a vineyard, stretch out his arms, draw the air in through his nose, and let the sweetness overwhelm him — his face full of hilarious and happy mischief.

"So much wine! So much wine!" Whenever he heard gurgling water, he imagined it was wine running through the ditches along the road.

And when wagons bounced past overloaded with grapes,

he gathered the fallen bunches from the ground. The grapes dripped onto the road and made it wet. He never washed the grapes, but he sucked them down to the pits, one by one. Then, since he was hungry too, he would eat the stems. It would have been a shame to throw them away. During the racking of the wine, he'd climb up onto the iron gates outside the cellars and get intoxicated on the pungent smell. Eventually, he'd be invited inside for a drink.

They let him drink so much that he'd have to prop himself up against the wall and hold his head high in order to keep the wine from pouring out his mouth. And then he fell asleep on the stoop of some roadside shrine, curled up in his rags and half dead.

He had long forgotten about his sister, Clelia, who ran a smoke shop with her husband in a village hidden in the forests along the border of Maremma and the lime pits of Siena. She hadn't heard from him and assumed he was still carting bricks. Then one day she decided to send him a package of dried chestnuts, and someone told her he had died.

Cecco's sister didn't believe it and decided to find out for herself. Within a few days, she had found a stagecoach that went to Siena via Coroncina, and she begged a ride.

She liked the feeling that she loved her brother — perhaps it was the first time she'd ever felt that. She remembered sleeping in the same bed with him when they were little, but the tenderness she was experiencing now was new and curious. She was the youngest. She had a square forehead with wrinkles running straight across it. Her face was thin and her smile would have been lovely if not ruined by a fold of flesh that just grew flabbier with time. She was robust and manly; she stood so straight her back swayed inward. Under her chin, she had a red birthmark.

When she arrived, she went right to the stall and let her

self in—thinking that at least she would see the mules. Instead, she found a dappled white horse. She looked at it from behind. Chewing its hay, the horse turned to look at her, and then turned back to its meal. She realized that the harness it was wearing was rather elegant. She smiled, and shook her head incredulously. *Goodness. Could Cecco have possibly become rich?*

She didn't know where he lived, so she left the stall in order to ask around. She approached a woman who was feeding porridge to a baby nestled in her arms.

"Where's Cecco?"

The woman looked at her slowly and unceremoniously from head to toe before answering.

"He hasn't been seen around town for a while now."

"But isn't this his stall?"

"His stall? Not for at least two years it hasn't been."

"Why? Where is he now?"

"You're asking me? He runs around like a mad dog."

And, by continuing to ask questions, Clelia gradually learned the whole truth. And then she was seized by a ridiculous panic. She was ashamed she'd come in the first place. She wanted leave town immediately, before he saw her. She didn't even want him to know she'd been there. But the woman headed off to call the neighbors, so they could meet Cecco's sister, too. She felt alone and sorry her husband was so far away. The coach wouldn't be back to pick her up before evening. What was she going to do all day long with these people staring at her that way? She started crying. A woman gave her a chair. She sat there, against the wall, in the sun, with a handkerchief on her head. She refused the invitations to come inside. She felt numb, and she worried she'd be sick. She kept her eyes lowered and wouldn't look at anyone. A pack of children hung around all day, singing and playing all their noisy games. She was hungry but didn't want to get up. Fortunately, she had a crust of bread left over in her apron pocket that she ate, one crumb at a time, and the children stopped playing to watch her chew. Her eyes seemed to be focused on nothing.

By evening, when she couldn't take it any longer and was about to fall asleep, her head lolling on the back of the chair, the coach arrived. The crack of the driver's whip woke her from her stupor; and he helped her up onto the carriage, because she was having difficulty finding where to set her feet. On the way home, she told the driver the whole story, about how upset she was. But then when she told her husband about it, she was critical of her brother. She blamed him for everything and couldn't think of any way to forgive him. She behaved this way, mostly because she didn't want to be reprimanded. But she took a certain pleasure in it, too, and kept on talking until she was sure her husband didn't think any less of her.

Cecco happened into town an hour after Clelia had left with the coach. As he walked, he balanced himself against the walls of the houses, stumbling only when there was an open door or a jutting harness hook.

The woman who Clelia had spoken to told him first, "Your sister was here, Cecco."

Remembering his sister, he suddenly felt like a different person, and he turned left and right to see her for himself. He didn't say a word, though. He just went a little pale.

"She's not here anymore. She just left on the coach."

So he said, "Why didn't you tell me before?"

"Where were you?"

"I've been asleep since this morning, over behind the house at the end of the village."

"Really? Santa Maria! You were so close, and you two didn't see each other!"

But he couldn't think anymore, and he responded, "I don't care!"

"She heard you were dead. That's why she came."

He either didn't hear, or he didn't understand. He kept looking down the main street, his eyes filled with the sweet tears of a drunk. He stopped thinking about his sister. He needed a glass of wine. The mad desperation of his desire spread over his face, and he felt tortured. Nothing meant anything to him anymore. He looked at the people standing around him as if they were hiding glasses of wine behind their backs. He looked at them with accusation and reproach. He looked at them with a dark and gloomy thirst.

But he was already drunk. Because, by now, it only took half a glass of wine to make him senseless. He went into a tavern where they were playing cards, *briscola* and *scopa*. He sat down to watch the game. The cards made his head spin, and he wanted to kiss each one as if it were a little statue of the Madonna.

Someone gave him a drink. He was beyond understanding anything, and it was only by instinct that he found the road to the oven where he slept. In any case, it was too dark to see two feet ahead.

He climbed up into the mouth of the oven and lay down. The heat he felt was too alive and suffocating, but he didn't have the strength to move, and it didn't occur to him to scream. He got thirstier and thirstier.

The next morning, they found him dead, almost baked, because the night before they had been making bread and so the oven was still hot.

(1919)

LIFE

■ ■ ■

Jacopo ran as fast as he could away from the farmhouse. His heart was pounding, and he couldn't breathe. He paused by the entrance of a neighboring farm, which had a low stone wall where he could hide if he needed to. But he was scared to stop for too long, and once he was rested, he started running again. The road led down, and the boy just wanted to get to the end of it. There was a tall hedge there, and then, he thought, he could make it to the other side.

Around a curve in the road, he almost ran directly into a Franciscan he knew, the same monk who had been tutoring him in reading and writing. The monk, named Father Ernesto, patted the boy's bare head, noticing that he'd forgotten his hat and that he'd grown terribly pale. But Jacopo leaped to one side in order to pass him and ran a few meters farther before he stopped again, picked up a rock, and hurled it at the monk. Then he fled.

The monk froze in surprise. He dusted off his tunic and then continued along his way, walking more slowly now. He came across the boy's father, who was carrying a cow-whip. He greeted the man with forced and false friendliness, turning red as he spoke.

"Signor Minello, what are you doing out in this sun?"

The farmer yanked his hat from his head, crossed his arms, and answered, "I'm waiting for my son to get back."

Minello didn't want to upset the monk. He had an instinctive respect for him, and he wouldn't have been able to suppress that if he wanted to. He liked the monk's beard, it was the color of red tobacco; and it was almost the same color as his tunic. The whole effect made him feel like a child, which made him angry, and so he began to curse, attempting to fight this helpless sense of obedience.

Father Ernesto was going to tell Minello about his son throwing a stone at him, but then changed his mind and decided to tell Jacopo's mother instead. It was entirely possible that Minello wouldn't bother to apologize for the boy's behavior and would just start hurling insults himself. The monk waved once more and continued on his way, walking more swiftly now.

Jacopo had eaten grapes off the vine. When his father found out, he'd grabbed the boy by the neck and dragged him into the threshing room. He threw him down by the carriage and went to get the whip from its place on a nail on the wall. But this time, rather than stay put, Jacopo escaped. If Minello caught him, he was going break his legs or his back. By now, he often thought that he was punishing the boy less than was necessary. Realizing that Jacopo wasn't going to come back, Minello sent two workers to look for him. The workers walked a bit down the road, then turned around and reported that they couldn't find him. But Minello wouldn't calm down. He wrapped the whip around his neck. He was going to thrash him that evening when he came home for dinner—and, if he didn't come back, at least he'd have to go without food.

Minello was a tall, thin man, his mustache had gone almost all white, his voice was nasal, he stuttered, and every night he got drunk. Then his face became swollen, and the only thing he could talk about was wine.

His wife tried to stay out of his way, and more and more often now would escape to her bed. But if she didn't get out in time, and he noticed that she was cowering or unhappy, he'd yell at her, try to trip her. Or else, he'd grab her by the arm and spin her around. If she laughed at that, then he'd accuse her of dipping into the wine herself. If she continued to make it apparent that she was suffering, he'd throw at her whatever first came into his hand.

"We don't want you here! No no! Get out! Go to bed. Go to your room!"

He'd snarl, throw punches at whoever came near him. If he found his wife praying, he'd completely lose his mind. He'd rage, bite his fists, and then turn on her with every intention of beating her.

Jacopo was fifteen years old, thin, and looked like his father. When these episodes happened, he'd get sick for two days at least, during which time he'd talk of nothing but getting away from the farm. He'd suffer panic attacks at night, but didn't talk about it, so no one ever knew. He had grown shy and always thought he was doing something wrong, even when he was talking to the farmhands or off on his own. It seemed like his father controlled everything and everybody, and there was no one over his father. And then he didn't even dare to look at him.

Ashamed of himself for having thrown a rock at the monk, Jacopo started to cry as he ran. When he got to the hedge, he just crawled inside. Then he began to wonder why he didn't get drunk too. Then at least, he reasoned, he'd feel some sort of satisfaction, doing exactly as he wanted. His fear turned to hysteria, and what had terrified him half an hour earlier made him laugh now. He giggled to himself, imagining how silly his father was, standing there waiting for him with his whip in hand. He was so content inside the hedge that he settled down, planning to stay there until he got bored. There was black soil around the base of the bush, teeming with grubs and earthworms; he entertained himself by grabbing handfuls of them and tossing them out from under the hedge. He was downright happy by the time he started back home. His father was already swaying so much that in order to talk, he had to rest one hand and then the other against the side of the house, turning his head constantly to make sure there wasn't anyone standing next to him. But when Jacopo saw the whip still wrapped around his father's neck, he realized he'd come back too soon. He started jumping and leaping playfully around the threshing room, trying to distract his father, managing to get the whip away from him. He shook the whip at a clutch of ducks, and they bumped into each other and tripped as they tried to get away. Ducks don't run very quickly anyway. So Jacopo slapped at the legs of the ones who'd fallen down. Then he put the whip back on its hook, laughing and keeping one eye on his father, who was shaking his head at the heavens. But the boy still didn't feel safe. In fact, when they both got back into the house, Minello dropped his head between his knees. The boy kept giggling, but felt like his heart was about to explode. Minello was shooting angry looks at him; Jacopo knew perfectly well why his father's eyes had grown brighter and clearer. The boy stopped laughing and tried to wriggle free. Holding him tighter, Minello grabbed for his hair, and then lazily punched him in the face. Jacopo's mother gathered her courage and pulled on Minello's arm, so he released the boy and hit her, kicking her over into the grain sacks. Jacopo fell to the ground, trembling and convulsing.

It was hot outside, too. Big, foamy clouds sat on the edge of the horizon, growing bigger and bigger, swelling up, and then glowing like a fire. The window was open and the silence from outside taunted Minello; he started swearing as if he'd provoked it. Dele, his wife, rushed into the other room, one hand holding back her hair, which had come untied, to get a cushion to put under Jacopo's head. Minello unfastened Jacopo's shirt. And, once the boy came around, he kissed him on the mouth. Dele had to pull him off. He'd gotten to the point where he didn't understand anything.

The next day, Minello stayed close to his son and wife; they returned his looks happily, really believing that he wasn't going to drink anymore. At the table he said, stuttering even more than normal, "Starting today, you should always put water in the wine pitcher!"

He looked at his wife as if he wanted to mock her disbelief and continued, "I don't want you saying that I'm difficult because I drink too much! That's a story you've made up, and it's got to stop. If it doesn't, I'll put both of you in your place. I can see now that you're all against me. But we need some good judgment around here."

The boy smiled, but the woman didn't look up from her cooking. Shaking her by the arm, he screamed, "You fool! Hey! I'm talking to you too! Actually, I'm talking more to you than to him!"

The woman answered under her breath, "I heard you."

"Good for you. Don't make me repeat myself."

She got up and added water to the wine. He let her, and once she put the flask back on the table, carefully placing it on top of a fig leaf so it wouldn't stain the tablecloth, he asked, "Where's the real wine?"

"There's another flask on the shelf."

"Go and get it for me."

Dele didn't want to obey him. She asked, "What do you want it for?"

"Did you really think that I would want to drink this concoction? I don't want to get warped like a piece of wood! Don't you know that too much water makes you warped?"

The boy stood up to leave the table.

"Sit back down, you. Or I'll clock you. Do I need your permission now?"

The woman opened the cabinet and brought out another flask, corked with a folded husk of corn. And, without considering the consequences, she said, "Drink it! Drink your poison!"

Minello shook his head and scratched his knee. After a while, he responded, "You're really the one who'll get poisoned, because you don't drink!"

"I'm happy with water."

"So why do you stick your nose in what doesn't concern you? Is this how you talk? I should teach you a lesson . . . with the cane. If there's a God, you'll be sorry. As if a woman should talk like that to me!"

The boy said, "Mamma's right!"

His nerves were still raw, and he was growing paler with every word. Then the woman dared to speak, because by now she knew that things were going the way they always did. "Watch out, or he'll have a fit again—like last night!"

"I'm the one who brings them on. Why should it happen again?" Jacopo turned to his mother, "It won't happen again, even if he's more horrible to you. It won't happen."

His mother looked at him tenderly and felt just as strongly as he did. Minello looked at both of them and started laughing. Then they laughed too, but without any control. They were scared and wanted to get away from him. They didn't want anything more to do with it. She said, "I don't know why you don't love us."

The words shook the boy up even more than before: he

stopped eating and started cleaning between his teeth with the prong of the fork. Then he poked his gum, and it started bleeding, so he went to the sink to rinse his mouth. Without turning around, his father asked, "What did you do to yourself?"

"Nothing."

"What do you mean nothing? So what are you doing?"

Holding a handkerchief to his lip, Jacopo answered, "I don't want you to hit Mamma!"

Dele said, "Be quiet. Don't worry about it!"

"No. I don't want to. He shouldn't hurt you!"

He lost control and dropped to the floor, rolling around on the sacks of grain.

Minello stared, "What are you trying to do to me?"

The boy looked around the room, his eyes stopping on the work tools, then turned to look at his father.

"You know I understand you!"

But Jacopo writhed on the ground, tearing at his shirt.

Minello said to his wife, "Make him get up. Can't you see what he's doing? I'm the one who's going to have to buy him a new shirt."

The woman started to cry; and the boy didn't take his eyes off his father, who was pretending not to notice. The woman said to her son, "Leave. Go and walk around the barn."

He answered, "I'm not leaving you alone!"

The man got heavily to his feet, pushed the boy out the door, closing it and locking it behind him. Then he sat back down at the table, his head between his hands. The woman continued crying. Minello said, as if she were to blame, "He thinks that I'm going to kill you now."

"Is this possibly the way I'm going to spend my whole life?"

"That's my fault too?"

"Let the boy back in."

"Think about it: how can he really think I want to kill you?"

The woman pulled herself together and answered quietly, "Because it's true."

He filled a glass of wine for himself and one for her. Then he took the flask and filled Jacopo's glass too. And ordered her, "Call him in."

The woman opened the door, but the boy didn't want to come back. He didn't want to make peace. But she dragged him inside by the collar of his shirt, telling him under her breath to obey. Without looking up, Minello shouted: "Drink! Both of you!"

The woman and the boy picked up their glasses and waited. Laughing and rubbing his eyes, Minello said, "There's nothing better than wine!"

And he made them drink until they were drunk, forcing them to drink every time he did, because if they loved him, he said, this was what they must do.

(1919)

VILE CREATURES

■ ■ ■

Non est creatura tam parva et vilis, quae Dei bonitatem non repraesentet 　　*—De Imitatione Christi*	No creature is too small or worthless to show the goodness of God 　　*—The Imitation of Christ*

It was just me and five girls. They sat together on one of the sofas. Pale and sickly Lina worked embroidery on green silk; her velvet dress was the color of cherries. Next to her, almost on top of her, sat Frenchie with her long blonde hair and sloppy painted mouth. Eva, the least homely of the group, showed off her cleavage; her stockings were nut colored, her dress was striped blue and white. Fanny wore a doll's dress, pink; her hair was loose and swept back with a ribbon; she was thin and heavily made up. Sara, a Jewess, had lots of hair; her feet were up on the sofa, and she held a book on her lap.

I had been astonished to note as I came up the stairs that I already felt not only satisfied, but also quite sober. I had chosen a seat off to one side, and I watched myself smoking a cigarette in the mirror on the opposite wall. Because I didn't have anything to say, and I wanted to behave like a practical person.

The girls looked me over, then continued to talk as if I weren't there.

Adjusting her stockings, Frenchie said, "What small ears you have, Lina! That's good luck, you know."

"Everyone tells me that. My mother had small ears, too."

"I have the biggest ears!" said Eva, laughing.

"I," said Fanny, "don't have anything from either my father or my mother."

Lina smoothed her embroidery over her knee. "It's been so long since I've seen my mother. I used to write to her before; but I stopped a few years ago."

"And I," said Fanny, "was very happy at home. My parents are well off. They have this sort of villa in Genoa, with a big garden. Back then, I was honest, I only had one lover, and he wanted to marry me."

"It's so cold tonight!" exclaimed Eva, her voice shrill and sweet.

Sara raised her head from her book to look at Eva, but didn't say a word.

Then Lina added, "My parents had a nice house, too, in Parma. My sisters weren't married yet when I left."

"I was happy in Leon," said Frenchie.

"I remember Venice," said Eva.

"But don't you remember anything about your families?" asked Fanny.

"Oh, lots of things," answered Lina.

"Me too!"

"Me too!" answered Eva and Frenchie in turn.

"If my parents knew how and where I live," continued Fanny, "they'd die. Poor things!"

"Doesn't that make you sad?" asked Frenchie.

"It's too late now."

I started to get embarrassed and tried to avert my gaze. But then Eva asked, as if she had been insulted, "Are you ashamed?"

Fanny shook her head, and said very seriously, "Anything but."

"If I found someone," said Lina, "who would take me away from here . . ."

"But that's never going to happen."

"Yeah."

Turning to Lina, I asked, "Would you love him?"

"Why not?" answered Eva.

"We get more attached than other women," explained Fanny.

"Can you believe that?" Eva asked me, as if it were a joke. So I laughed.

But Fanny wanted to convince me, "On my word, if I knew you loved me . . . that someone loved me, I'd never do him wrong."

Sara stopped reading, as if she didn't want to be made fun of.

"You don't know about me. When I was sixteen, I went to church and gave confession. I never imagined I'd end up like this. I swear it isn't my fault."

Sara didn't answer; she just readjusted her position on the sofa and turned back to her book. Frenchie smoothed her hips, shook her golden hair, and said, "I believe you."

"Yes. You understand better than the others."

Eva and Lina laughed loudly. Then Lina said, "What are you bragging about? I have three sisters, and I'm the only one who's different. They'd take me if I wanted to go home. But I wouldn't go back there to save my life. My father is well known and respected in Parma. He's a gentleman. He always used to take me riding with him on a little horse, because he didn't want me going out alone. My sisters were jealous, they wouldn't even look at me at the end. They'd be happy if they knew about how I live. But I try to hide it all—out of respect for my father. If you only knew how much I love him. I keep his picture with me in my trunk; and I hope I'll get to see him again one day, before he dies."

Then Lina swore. She said an obscene word. So Eva said,

"I don't have anyone left . . . I only remember that my mother wanted me to be a teacher . . . But I didn't study . . . I had a baby girl when I was only thirteen. Then I had to leave town because my mother wanted to shut me up in a convent . . . Then I ended up in a correctional institute . . . but not for long, because I managed to escape and met someone who took me in for four years. I thought I was going to die when he started to get bored. I was a singer, too, but I didn't like that. I was a singer for two years, but I don't have the right kind of voice."

Then, as if she didn't want to seem less than the others, Frenchie said, "I've been all over Europe. My mother is the only one still living, and I send her as much as I can every month because she's taking care of my son, who just had his communion. I've never seen him. He thinks I'm dead. They've been telling him from the start that I went to America with his father."

Fanny said, "I never had children. But I'd thank God if I did have one."

"Why is that?" I asked.

"Because everyone needs someone to love."

Fanny's answer was curt, almost resentful. And she went on, as if she were scolding me, "You see me dressed like this, and you don't think that I'm just like other women. When I think that I could be taking a walk in my garden today, and be near my family, I lose patience. It makes me miserable. I've done everything I could to forget, and I wish I could. I used to cry in despair at the beginning, because I just couldn't accept all of this. Now, even though I've gotten used to it, I envy people who aren't like me. But no one's ever come to help me."

"Why don't you go home?"

Fanny's tone was almost like a dare, "Do you really think

they'd take me? You can see what I do for a living just by looking at my face. And if someone were to say something about it, the slightest mention, I'd have to leave again. I know exactly how they'd react to seeing me again. And they're right. I have to think about it first."

Eva wasn't laughing anymore. She said, "You should have thought about whether you were tough enough before."

Lina answered, the sarcasm in her voice was insulting, "If I'm not mistaken, we've all had the same luck."

Frenchie asked Sara, "What are you reading?"

"A novel."

"Is it good?"

"So-so," answered Sara, careful not to reveal how she felt about the book.

"Who's the author?"

"I don't know."

"Why don't you look?"

"You're so annoying. Why don't you leave me alone! I find it very strange that you can't seem to leave me alone."

"Let me see the title."

Sara handed her the book, and Frenchie read the title. Then she said with disdain, "I've read that, too." And she shrugged.

Sara went back to reading. Lina folded her piece of cloth. She had embroidered a shamrock. Eva asked her, pretending to care, "Why don't you make one for me?"

"Tomorrow."

"Me, too," said Frenchie, knowing she was just making conversation.

"You, too."

"I'm already tired," said Eva, leaning her head back against the wall.

Without meaning to, I started thinking about my father and mother too. How quickly time had passed; how much effort it took to breathe. I looked at the embroidery, and Lina noticed. She smiled pleasantly at me. I had actually forgotten what kind of place I was in, and that made me sad. I saw that Fanny's fingers, although they were nicely shaped, looked like crab claws when they moved. And I couldn't tell whether the hair hanging over her shoulders was really hers. Sara was hiding her face behind her hands, and Frenchie had turned toward Eva.

My impression of my memories was painful and kept getting more so. I couldn't figure out why everything seemed tragic—as if someone had been murdered right in front of our eyes. As if our souls were shocked. I wondered which one of the five girls I might feel closest to; but then I couldn't find any differences between them. Fanny was the youngest and maybe she was the one with the most goodness in her. But I liked Lina, too. Her embroidery made me imagine her house in Parma. For each one of them, there was something that kept me from being completely disgusted or even feeling indifferent. I grew more and more willing to defend them. I was absolutely exalted by these feelings. I wanted to confide in them, too, but I couldn't. I never would have been able to talk about myself and my family the way they did. We shared the same nostalgia, the same regrets. Home was far away, and I was suddenly happy to have this unexpected and spontaneous sense of affinity. I had never felt as willing with my whole soul, nor ever felt as well understood, as I did with those five girls. Their conversation obliged me to be good and respectful. I would have protected them from anyone. I was overcome by the desire to have them understand everything I was feeling. So Fanny, who was the first to notice this, smiled delicately and said, "What are you thinking about?"

"Me? . . . Nothing."

"You seem so serious."

"Should we sing something?" asked Lina.

Fanny was curious, but didn't want to irritate me. That didn't stop her from feeling confident enough to tell me, "You and I communicate with just our eyes. I'm not saying that to make you start thinking about me—don't start thinking that—we're all equal in here."

Frenchie said, "I have no idea what's going on in your head."

To which she answered, "You think I don't understand people?"

Eva, though she was the most frivolous, looked at me as if she were trying to confirm what Fanny had said; Lina just stared at me in bewilderment. Even Sara looked up at me, but her face still bore the traces of whatever she had been thinking about while reading. She furrowed her brow slightly, and it almost seemed like she wanted to close her book. But then she yawned, and not having anything to say, she started reading all over again—less attentively than before. You might even say that her ears were cocked for what was being said now and that she was following the conversation in her head. Fanny didn't take her eyes off me, which made me so embarrassed I wanted to be alone. Who knew what Lina was trying to say? But more than once, she seemed to want to say something. And Frenchie, who was sitting next to her, snickered every time she saw Lina's lips move.

"What's so funny?" asked Eva, because she wanted to be the only one laughing. Instead of answering her, Frenchie burst out and made sure her laughter lasted longer. This put Eva back into a good mood, even though she still couldn't figure out who was on her side. So she tested them all, looking at each girl, turning up the corners of her mouth. Finally, bowing her head almost down to her chest, she kept on smiling silently.

"I cried a lot this morning," said Fanny.

"Every day, it's somebody else's turn. I cried yesterday," answered Lina.

"But I cried for almost an hour, when I was waiting for the hairdresser."

"I cried two hours, before dinner."

"Do you really think that's a lot?" asked Frenchie.

"I didn't say that," answered Fanny.

"What are you saying? If any of you knew how much I cry."

Eva looked at the tips of her fingernails, then at her pale satin, mouse-colored slippers. Sara shrugged it all off, then said, "It would be better if you could all try to keep our secrets private. Other people don't really care."

"I always tell the truth," declared Fanny. "It might be wrong, but I can't keep quiet."

Eva looked over at her, laughing that laugh of hers — rising and falling, like her voice.

By that point, I had come to feel affection for all five of them. Within me, they were purified. And maybe I had learned something I didn't know before. It was a new feeling, and I promised myself never to lose it. I suspected they wouldn't believe me, even if I told them I was scared. Maybe I could have told Fanny, if we were alone. I could talk to her, because she was my girlfriend then, my sister too. But wouldn't Eva be offended? And why would I prefer Fanny to Frenchie or Lina? Why couldn't I make Sara look away from her book — Sara, who wasn't giving me the respect that I wanted for all the sincerity I was feeling in their regard. Why wouldn't she meet me halfway?

The door opened, and an elderly man with a long, well-groomed mustache said hello and removed his hat.

My dream disappeared like a soap bubble, leaving only indignation and resentment for this man. I left immediately, so I wouldn't have to be in the same room with him.

(1918)

THE IDIOT

. . .

Fiocco, the idiot — thirty years old and still fighting with the other children because they wouldn't leave him alone in the courtyard to cut figures out of playing cards with a pair of scissors — fell into a deep sleep.

It was two in the afternoon. And not one of the residents of the five-story apartment building was looking out their windows, and Fiocco's parents weren't home. Most of the men were still at work in their stores or offices, and the children and women were napping on account of the heat. Sounds of servants working in the kitchens drifted through the windows left open just a crack. That was all.

Fiocco dreamed and even believed that the King of Spades had married the Queen of Hearts. They had always been his two favorite cards.

So he asked permission to enter their domain and tell them how happy he was for them.

I know you love each other very much! But I've known that for a long time. Whenever I shuffled the deck and you two were next to each other, I was sure I saw some kind of movement. That would make me stop playing. Now, how come I find you alone together here in this pile of trash? Tell me everything. What are you doing in there?

The two cards had been rained on and then dried out by

the sun. Fiocco loved them no matter how faded they were. And though he would rather talk with the Queen, the King was more willing to talk to humans. Looking right into Fiocco's eyes, the King of Spades began to speak:

"The only card games you know how to play are gin rummy, slapjack, and *briscola*, so let me tell you a little about what happens when you go off to bed and your family plays without you. You'll be surprised by what a great memory I have. Cecilia and Laura are your sisters, Arturo is Laura's fiancé, Matilde is your mommy, Ugo is your father, Enrico and Giulio are friends of the family. And I'll tell you something else that you should know but would never figure out on your own, the Ace of Clubs was in love with Cecilia. The Ace of Hearts, one of my own subjects, was in love with Laura. The Three of Diamonds was Arturo's good friend, and the Queen of Clubs was in love with Arturo. The Jack of Hearts and the Jack of Diamonds both liked Matilde. Neither the Three of Clubs nor the Three of Spades liked your father much, and none of the cards ever wanted to be in his hand. The Queen of Diamonds was crazy about Enrico. Pay attention, so you don't get confused. We cards know more about what's going on during a game than the people who are playing. It would be quite impossible for me to explain what lengths we go to in order to help our patrons in the game. In the end, of course, we have no control over the draw, and if we're lucky to wind up together, we have to refrain from expressing either joy or disappointment. You humans have no idea! And for what it's worth, neither my esteemed wife nor I have ever taken sides against anyone. When we are placed face down in the dark, the most we can do is try to sneak an embrace. How could you possibly understand our love? Not even the moths dancing in the light understand us!

"Once, convinced she was doing the Three of Diamonds

a favor, the Queen of Clubs tried desperately to make Arturo win. Oh, what tension this created every time Arturo and Laura—your sister, Arturo's fiancé—touched. The Queen was so jealous of Laura! The Queen kept slipping from Laura's grasp and finally fell face up on the table so that the other players could see her. The Three of Diamonds called in all his debts in order to please the Queen and even won the assistance of my esteemed lady. On the third round, the Queen of Clubs fell to Cecilia, your other sister. And throughout the entire game, Cecilia nibbled on her cards — you know how people do that when they are deep in thought, waiting for their turn. The Queen of Clubs was so caught up in the game her heart was racing. And Cecilia is such a care- less player. She puts all her energy into building up points. Very well. The card understood right away that both she and Cecilia were rooting for Arturo. Fortunately, the Ace of Clubs, who I've explained was in love with Cecilia, hadn't been played yet. And so the Queen still had a chance to be useful. But Arturo loves Laura, and he wasn't paying atten- tion to all these goings-on.

"Maybe it was intuition on Cecilia's part, but she figured out that Arturo needed the Queen of Clubs, and so she played the Queen. The Ace of Clubs was in Matilde's hand and doing everything in his power to get away. Matilde stared at him, undecided about which card to play, when sud- denly, as if obeying an order, she put down the Ace. Cecilia jumped in her seat with joy! Arturo called *briscola*, racked up the most points, and won the game.

"Not only is Arturo a nice boy and one of the best auto- mobile mechanics around, but in your home he's the only hope left that your father won't completely destroy the family. Laura and Arturo's wedding represents your parents' chance for the future—otherwise there would be no reason at all for them to stay together. You know, sometimes it's better for families like yours to just break up and let everyone go their separate ways in the world. It would mean so much less fighting and less pain — much more serenity and spiritual strength. And you barely understand what I'm telling you. I certainly don't know what miracle is working on your brain today so that you're able to comprehend all this information. Of course, you really only have fun when you've got your hands on those scissors. Oh! Then, your eyes — how your eyes shine! You must suffer so from being barely able to think!

"If I were to tell you to kill yourself, you would do it without a second thought. It's strange how you only understand things that please you, or things you'd like to do anyway. Anything else, you think with satisfaction, isn't an instruction worthy of one of your paper dolls!

"You also want revenge on Laura because her shoes aren't made of gray leather like yours. You look at her shoes with such hatred. You spy on her through the keyhole while she's dressing. You know all of your family's biggest secrets. They don't have the slightest idea how much you know. If you were able to talk, you might even tell them exactly how many times in the past five years your mother has darned her secondhand stockings.

"And still you are surprised when your mother kneels by your side and prays that you'll get better. Don't you know why you grind your teeth and get suspicious of anyone who comes to comfort her when she cries? Even if it's Cecilia? Anytime you're the slightest bit happy, all you want to talk about is how many bricks there are in the walls of each room of the apartment. Because you counted them! And no one knew you were doing it! For ten years you kept the first little bunch of hair Cecilia ever left in the teeth of her comb, and then you gave it to her. You found the hair in the courtyard.

You drool for a whole day over the ends of thread your mother throws out after sewing. You stuff your fingers in your mouth and then let your anger build up for more than a month.

"So why should I tell you all this? Because I know you want Arturo to marry Cecilia instead of Laura. Cecilia loves you, and she's a good sister to you. Laura has betrayed you. She never dries the spit from your mouth when you moan because you're feeling even worse and you can't understand anything anymore. Cecilia would never leave your side, and she never wanted them to put you into the asylum.

"Do you know where you are now? You're in my kingdom. Watch that you don't step on the feet of my beloved wife. It is true though, my dear Fiocco, that you did try once to throw Laura into the well! If she hadn't dropped the bucket and grabbed on to the pulley, you might have drowned her. Don't you remember? You don't even know how to talk, but you're so strong you could have won that fight. You take pleasure in reminding her about it. Why is that? Especially when you are all at the table. You'll raise your hand and point toward the well. You laugh and point two times, just to show her how easy it would be to finish her off. Honestly, you don't think she'd last a day if they left you alone with her! You plucked the feathers off those two turtledoves while they were still alive. Did you do that because they were her birds? Is that why you stabbed Arturo with a knife? Fortunately, you only pricked the palm of his hand. Now Laura has gone and asked Cecilia why she defends you. Your sisters wouldn't even be sharing a bed anymore if Laura wasn't going to be married soon. But you still want to kill her. I know how much you hate her. And I'll tell you another thing. if you did manage to kill her, it would be because you've figured out that you will have to take her by surprise before she has time to turn on the lights. But Arturo will never marry Cecilia. Then you will end up beating Cecilia in order to punish yourself. It will go on like that until your parents' friends, Enrico and Giulio, have you locked up with all the other sick people.

"It's all inevitable because your drunkard father secretly thinks it's funny. He wants you to kill your mother. But it isn't important what he wants. One glance from her and you fall to your knees. If you did kill Matilde—just like that, for no reason and without any goading from him—he would steal a million lire and give it to you to make you rich. Does that make you laugh? Be careful you don't drool all over my wife's dress. Get a hold of yourself! Then Enrico and Giulio would make your father marry the woman they are both in love with, and they would never leave his side.

"Storms are the only thing you're really scared of now. You even run to Laura during a storm, but then you start torturing her as soon as the thunder stops. You should keep in mind that the Queen of Hearts is always watching you with her steely eyes, cold and steely like a newly slaughtered lamb. She will do anything to protect Laura. You're crazy! Don't you realize that you think her crown is made of gold and her dress of silk? You think of her the way others think of God. But the mere sight of my black beard disheartens you.

"Do you know what people say about Laura and Cecilia? They call them 'the sisters of that idiot.' Your sisters have heard them. At first, they thought they were being insulted unjustly. They were hurt by how mean people could be, how shameless and cynical. That kind of talk made them feel like the whole family shared your deformity. They felt like everyone knew about them, no matter where they went. At first, they even thought somehow that they were idiots too. And don't forget how much you all resemble each other physically. Neither of them was ever able to explain that. They feel chained to your sickness, and that will definitely make them age prematurely.

"Your mother loves you because she blames herself for your unhappiness; every day it gets worse. You are part of her, and she feels responsible for everything you do—such is motherhood. Your sisters avoid you because you smell so bad it's almost nauseating. You horrify them. They even teased you themselves when they were younger. The more you didn't act like the other children at school, the more your own sisters would tease you. Every so often, they decide you are more animal than human and try to pretend you aren't their brother.

"Now you have foolish dreams. Do you really think you're going to be a millionaire someday, a billionaire even? Tell me you don't believe that! Do you know what makes Cecilia's heart race? She is going to be Arturo's sister-in-law, and she is in love with him. She knows he will be unhappy and won't fall in love with her after Laura dies. I have no idea how she knows all that, but it torments her. She even cries for your mother, because of how much Ugo makes her suffer.

"You had already gone to bed, or rather, they had sent you to bed, and Cecilia had been in to help you off with your shoes. Ugo came home and punched his wife. His two friends, who never say a word, stood back pretending they hadn't seen anything. Arturo and Laura were in front of the window, behind the curtains. Cecilia had work as a sales clerk in a clothing store back then. She was in the kitchen. Matilde cowered and buried her head in the crook of her arm. Arturo stepped forward. Naturally, Laura was begging him to defend your mother. When Ugo is drunk, he laughs just like you and walks just like you. He takes your mother and shoves her into the kitchen, knocking her against Cecilia, making Cecilia spill boiling water all over her hands. Her hands still haven't healed. Arturo grabs your father and tries to hold him back against the wall. Laura cries. Your father is infuriated and takes a knife from the table and hits her over the head with the handle. Arturo uses all his strength to hold him back. But the friends are on your father's side, and they set him free.

"The party lasted until morning. They drank five more bottles of wine and then, having finished the game, threw all the cards, along with the table and chairs, out of the window into the courtyard where you found us. Arturo and the women locked themselves in the kitchen to tend their injuries.

"Your father wanted to drag you from your sound sleep and set you up on a kind of throne on the sofa in the living room. Instead, he and his friends came in to gawk at you, and they poured wine all over you and your sheets, trying to get you drunk, too. It wouldn't have taken much before your bed went up in flames.

"Whatever you do, don't think that your father loves you. When you were twenty years old, he tried to hack off your fingers with those very same scissors you're holding now. And don't you remember what he did to you when you were a little boy? You were all living in the country then, and hadn't moved into this house yet. You fell into a fountain, so he put you into the oven that was still hot from baking bread to dry you out. And he laughed so hard! They had to drag him away and explain to him that you might die and he would be condemned for murder. In the meantime, your mother sneaked you out of the oven and saved you. But he never did believe that you had been in any real danger. And even though you don't understand people when they talk, you know he bragged about the whole affair and insisted that cooking you in the oven would have done you good. You make him laugh when he's drunk. That's all there is to it.

"The next morning, your father didn't have the guts to show his face. That's why he still hasn't come home. Arturo is too good to abandon Laura. Now, leave us cards in peace."

But Fiocco answered, *Since I can talk to you without saying anything and without needing the usual words, I beg you to do something to keep me from killing my sister. Would I really do something like that? It's true that I feel very clever and have no need for revenge, but my cleverness is very tempting. It would give me great pleasure to kill her. But if the Queen of Hearts doesn't want me to kill her, you'll have to turn Laura into a card and then tell her not to hate me anymore. You said that all this is inevitable and has nothing to do with me. And I confess that when I am around her . . . But why does she have to be my sister?*

The Queen of Hearts responded, "I hope a roof falls on your head before you have a chance to commit this crime."

Fiocco started moaning, and he moaned for a long time. Eventually, his mother looked out into the courtyard and saw him. She came down and called his name right into his ear, over and over, trying to make him stop crying. Fiocco finally stood up, but he wanted to bring the two playing cards with him and cut them up into little pieces.

Through the kitchen window of another apartment came the sound of a maid, laughing.

(1914)

TO DREAM OF DEATH

...

Regina, the lame gardener who worked at the bishop's villa, had become one with her book on dreams.

She bought it one morning after managing to get out of paying taxes on the eggs, and now, when she didn't have time to leaf through it, she kept it in a kitchen drawer next to the gardening shears, the scissors, and the twine for binding flowers. Her sole ambition was to understand and interpret her dreams by herself. A good dream stuck in her head all day long, and after eating, napping, lingering over the dishes, she washed her hands thoroughly and opened her book.

She didn't start off by looking up her dream; there were so many enchanting pages to go through first, especially the ones with the illustrations.

And when she did find her dream in the book, she felt sudden satisfaction, like true love, because then she was sure she had remembered it correctly and hadn't "been mistaken," like the other ladies who didn't even know how to tell their dreams properly. Her heart would start pounding because, before reading the interpretation, she wanted to make sure she had read right and that she'd really dreamed that dream. Even Regina knew that the desire to have a good dream might keep you from remembering the dream honestly. Only as a final step did she let herself read. More than anything else she did, this pleasure was one she didn't share with anyone.

Once, she dreamed about five dead people filing past her. Other people, dressed in black, were leading them away. And she was in a city she had definitely never been in before.

The dream frightened her. She already had the idea planted in her head that she was going to die soon, and this dream didn't make her feel any more peaceful. She could sense her own existence waning, becoming less important—even to her—replacing itself with an dull pain.

Wasn't the row of five corpses a sign sent to prepare her for the end?

Flipping through the pages of her dream book would be useless! She didn't even bother opening it. As nighttime drew near she marveled that she still had an appetite and had eaten so well despite her worries. What was the dream really about? Death? Or health and long life?

And then, in a moment of lucidity, she asked herself, What is the meaning of five pallbearers? Could it mean five more days? Five more weeks? Five more months? Seasons? Years?

Five became a sacred number, a magic number. It appeared everywhere she looked, and it frightened her. There were five bouquets to wrap, five eggs to retrieve from the piles of straw in the chicken coop at sunset, five people coming to visit, five beggars asking for charity.

There was a sour taste in her mouth when she woke the next day, and she decided it would be best to just go on with her life as if nothing had happened. And at once she felt a sense of solitude wrap around the villa—she could almost hear its footsteps, padding on cotton slippers, so delicate you couldn't see them. It came into the garden; it took her. And the dog didn't even bark! Everything was silent. The frame around the tightly locked door seemed to groan under the weight of the intrusion: all of it, growing more powerful. It was a solitude made of steel, buried more deeply than a gravestone, rooted more deeply than a whole mountain, more than those mountains — the same ones she saw every evening on the horizon, over where the sun set.

She prayed aloud in order to reassure herself she had a voice. Then she dressed and left the house. It was as if she were being followed, and she kept checking over her shoulder. She called to the dog, "Pallino! Go fetch! Look everywhere!"

The dog sniffed the air and headed off, but he came right back to her side, wagging his tail and watching her attentively. In the end, she decided to get everything ready for when they would come and discover her, dead. The bishop was away (at the diocese), so she left him a note, written on a large piece of paper, carefully ironed flat with a smooth stone, listing all the bills left to be paid. It was only a few lire, because at the end of the month she usually sent him his share of the profits from the sale of his flowers, and they were only a week into the new month.

She checked everything; she swept the main building, dusted, closed, and locked all the doors. She hid the keys under an old bug-infested table by the front door and wrote where she had put them in her note. Then she sealed it with wax and burned her finger in the process.

She organized all the garden tools, lined up the flower-pots in the greenhouse, and she waited.

On the third day, she looked out over the garden wall and saw a driver she knew. She gave him the dog, sure she had found a good home for him. She didn't give Pallino away out of spite, but because she was worried about what would happen to him after she was dead.

She waited with a courage that brought clarity and new innocence to those blue eyes of hers, hidden as they always were under her wrinkled lids. She prayed twice that evening, lit all the oil lamps—deciding that, at best, she would finish the oil. There was no one for her to leave it to anyway, and she had always been very good to the poor.

But while she was clearing out the drawer where she kept her dream book, she felt her heart rise and tumble. What was she going to do with her book?

She took it out, and first she wrapped it in newspaper, then in a piece of cloth, and then she went to tuck it in between the ceiling crossbeams, convinced that no one would take it from there, unless the building collapsed or they took it down.

From that point on, there was nothing left to do.

But what illness was going to kill her? She didn't even have a headache. Only it seemed to her that she was outside of herself and that she was dreaming.

The fourth day was the hardest. She wept from morning till night, thinking about her youth, her marriage, her relatives, her friends—thinking of every lovely thing, like bright, peaceful days. There had been so many.

She could see the monastery clearly from her garden, and toward nightfall, it just so happened that a monk came by to ask her for a lemon, because one of the brothers felt unwell. She picked half a dozen for him and then asked if she could come for confession.

It wasn't a convenient hour for the monk, but out of a sense of respect he didn't tell her not to. She dressed in her best clothes and went to confession. When she spoke, she didn't even attempt to hide her fear of death and why she feared it. The monk absolved her and told her not to believe in dreams. But that advice, though given in the form of scripture, could never surpass the strength of Regina's will. And she was deeply hurt that even a religious would abandon her at her death.

She put this same trust in the existence of God; it was even more clear and definitive. And that evening, as she went to bed, she felt almost enthusiastic, lost to her dream.

The next day, she didn't get up for breakfast. Two hours after the stroke of noon, suddenly, without suffering, without even noticing, she died. The force of her will to die guided her into death.

(1916)

THE LOVERS

■ ■ ■

He awoke at the break of dawn. Augusta had already been up for a quarter of an hour and was busy clearing off the table.

He said to her, "Why don't you come over here and give me a kiss?"

But then he started feeling guilty and didn't dare insist. The woman didn't move from where she was. It wasn't very bright out yet, and although he was embarrassed, he marveled at the fact that he was up so early. When she was looking the other way, he stretched so that he would at least have something to do. Then he went to the window and opened it.

There was a thick, heavy fog forcing its way through the streets of Rome. The crosses on the steeples seemed to hover above the rooftops, separating themselves and standing out against the clear, bright sky.

The woman was still pale from sleep, and her braided hair had come loose over her half-naked shoulders. The braids were ugly, but her shoulders were lovely, and he stood motionless behind her, watching them while she continued cleaning.

Then, guessing what he was feeling, she turned slightly and said to him, "You could start loving me now, but it's too late."

He knew she was right, but didn't want to lose her, so he answered, "That's not true!"

She turned abruptly to face him, and so he wouldn't have to lower his eyes to avoid hers, he pretended he'd been thinking about something else and hadn't understood. He was half convinced she would be kind, but he didn't want to compromise himself by asking. Because then, he would be forced to admit the truth. Even though she hadn't asked anything of him, he was prepared to become emotional — although he no longer felt capable of really loving her. He took her face in his hands and stroked it, but she pulled away and tossed a braid off her neck, sending it flying. She said to him, "I don't want to discuss how you've behaved with me."

She was right, and he didn't like it. He almost envied her. He answered, "You're right, and you can scold me."

"It's too late. I told you."

He moved closer to her, but she pushed him away and put her hand over his mouth. He said, "You let me kiss you last night! And you kissed me back."

"And I have never behaved otherwise with you."

"Then why are you acting different this morning?"

"You need to feel sorry for what you've done. Leave. Please go now."

Instead, he grabbed her shoulders and forced her to stand there and hug him. She grew even more resolute and pulled her face away. Then he let her go. He was too angry, and yet he agreed with her. She was better than he was. So he waited, his head lowered, for her to say a kind word. He was sorry that he hadn't loved her. But since he was sorry, and she must realize that, he didn't understand why she couldn't forgive him. She must be able to forgive him.

The fog was lifting. The gray and turquoise church

domes hung there between the terraces and roofs. The flowers on the balcony dripped as if it had just rained.

The woman was less pale, but her pain was visible. Her hands made mistakes. He began to suffer, and he said, "You must forgive me."

The woman started and looked at him. He had a sincere voice; he was almost begging. Then she put her hand on his shoulder, but she didn't smile. He caressed her naked arm, ran his fingers along her elbow up her arm. She didn't want his caresses, although she stood firmly where she was. He understood, and so he stroked her hand. He felt like he would be able to be good to her and love her; but he couldn't say it. She guessed what he was thinking and said, "You don't know yet whether you are sorry or not."

He blushed, sweetly. But that blush was hurtful to the woman. He saw her mouth twist slightly. It was the right time to kiss her! First, he needed to make her his again. Which is why he continued watching her, with an instinct almost to diffidence. But she kept her face there, so that he would understand how he must love her. Her head wasn't beautiful now—with those braids—but he remembered how he had liked her the night before. He didn't need to see her twisted mouth to know that it hadn't been like that when he had desired her. Her face seemed bloated under thick, flabby skin, and her eyes were like two furrows cut into the ground. Her eyelids were red; she was tired and beaten. But he remembered the radiant beauty of her face the night before; how the shadow of her chin fell over her almost fully exposed breasts. Now he could only see that splendor in the depths of her eyes—those eyes he didn't want to look into. And he didn't feel that her soul belonged to him anymore! He had been unfaithful, and she was right. But she suffered like him. Or was she self-righteous and proud? He couldn't figure it out, because he just didn't like how she was treating him. Even though he thought it was useless, he stroked her hand. He saw the natural vigor return to her face, but it was a stern vigor. Her mouth was closed tight. And maybe he would never kiss it again. A mouth that had never kissed anyone, that had never kissed anything. She straightened up unconsciously, arching her neck out from her lovely shoulders, from the nightgown he was not worthy of touching; because he had been unfaithful to her. It seemed that even her nightgown knew and wanted him to leave! Looking at her in that way made him feel small. He felt like he should become another person. Since this idea gave him the sensation of unforgettable happiness, he said to her, "If you want, I'll go now, but I'll come back later."

He wanted to be clear and bright like the sky. He wanted to have the simple urgency of the sky, because he knew once the fog lifted off Rome, he wouldn't be capable. He continued, "I promise you."

But she answered, "When I was alone and suffering from loneliness, you never came to me. You only came when you wanted me. Isn't that true?"

He was sorry to admit that it was almost true; and he wanted to lie, because he loved her too much and wanted to be loved again right away. But maybe this hope was vain, and he looked jealously out the window at the Roman domes, illuminated now by the rising sun. There wasn't much time left. His love should be like the brightening sky. The woman was there, and her beauty was growing more assertive. Soon she would be like she was the night before and like she was every day: more beautiful than when he had fallen in love with her. Because it was her beauty that had always been the most important thing. He never thought that a woman like that could suffer—even over him. He thought about it, and it still seemed incredible. So why couldn't she explain herself better? Why hadn't she talked to him about it the way all other women did? But she said, "You knew I was suffering!"

"No."

"Did you think that I didn't need you?"

Feeling himself so much smaller than she was, he blushed until his cheeks burned. Then, beneath his blush his true feelings began to come clear. He was anxious to speak, and he would have expressed his feelings, if she hadn't kept on talking as though she had some right. "You won't come back now. You won't ever see me again."

There was great confusion in his head, and he didn't know how to answer. He was seized by sudden anger and thought he would explode. But all he did was stop stroking her hand.

"I suffered too much."

And not finding any excuse, he asked, "Why did you let me sleep in your bed, then?"

"So that you would know the woman you lost. I wanted to punish you in this way. This morning you will suffer. It's what you deserve. I knew you would be sorry to leave me this morning. While, until last night, I hadn't seen you for almost a month. If you do love me, you've got to realize the harm you've done: done to yourself most of all."

"But I thought you loved me, since you let me sleep with you!"

"It's true. I love you. But we must never see each other again. I was thinking about it last night while you were sleeping. And I can't come up with any more excuses for you. The only reason you came to see me was because it was convenient for you."

In fact, he had slept through the night without worrying about her in the least. But why hadn't she sent him away that very same night then? Why had she let him stay? He was suspicious of what she said, and at the same time he felt humiliated by her refusal to give the night they'd spent together some meaning. Then he turned on her, thought harshly of her, judged her behavior as base lust. Why would he want to love her if she had already proved she was that kind of woman? Why didn't she feel any shame?

He didn't take his eyes off her face. And he watched her eyes grow brighter, shiny. He thought he loved her irresistibly, and that he would never be able forget her. His voice was nervous and anxious. He said, "Well if I must go, then I'll go right now."

She was hurt, but she contained herself and answered almost with disdain, and without looking up, "Go ahead."

Before opening the door, he looked back at her and wanted to embrace her. Almost against his will he opened the door instead. He looked at her once again, and disappointed that she didn't say anything to him, he left, closing the door behind him.

Then the woman sat down and started to braid her hair. She set her hairbrush on the table with trembling hands; slowly, slowly, not making a sound, she fell to her knees. Her whole face cried more tears than ever could have fallen from her eyes. She rubbed her eyebrows lightly and looked at the bed. Then she pulled her head up and gathered her hair in her hands. She released it and leaned over to pick up a bit of cigarette. She put it in the ashtray. She was alone again; and in order to be loved, she had uselessly given him the pleasure of her beauty.

While down in the street, not daring to look up at the walls of the houses, he went to the Tiber to drown himself.

(1915–19)

ONE EVENING, ON THE BANKS
OF THE TIBER

■ ■ ■

Have you ever been in love with someone else's lovers, if only by virtue of hearing them spoken of? I have. At least, I've felt affinity for these women—something beyond just friendship. I only hear their words repeated and stories of how they love, and through the confidences of my friends, these women are brought to life. I've wanted to meet them. And then they disappear, too soon. Though the real ones, who belong to us, who interest us, end even sooner, and we try to forget. Memories of these other women, however, are enduring, possessed with a sense of eternity.

I ate at a trattoria in Rome every day. Many of my friends ate there, too, painters and sculptors mostly.

Giovanni Fossi was among those friends, and one evening after dinner, we joined arms and went for a stroll and a cigarette along the banks of the Tiber. We ended up under the Bridge of Sant'Angelo after having first passed through I don't know how many dark, narrow alleys, gathering places for the kind of women who smiled at us—though you couldn't tell if they were smiling or scarred.

It was foggy, and the first pillar of the bridge—where the

statues are—was lit up. The rest of the bridge stood dark in the night.

The water was an angry violet, cut across by four long electric reflections. The balustrade before us was black. Further down, the river was grimy, green. The water flowed in all directions, wrinkles over its surface.

The remains of the old iron bridge were still standing, like some sort of elliptical cage. In the distance, new streetcars passed over the Vittorio Emanuele Bridge, which led almost right into the courthouse—a gigantic, brilliant rectangle, illuminated with electric lights. Some boys were throwing stones at the scaffolding that was built when the old bridge had been dismantled.

My friend was a young man, twenty-four years old. He had the baby-smooth skin of an old man, feverish eyes, and he was very thin.

The brisk evening was good for both of us. We liked looking at the silent, gray, dark houses along the Tiber. There were electric lanterns over the stairwells in some of them that we could see through the open windows.

Fossi held my arm tightly, and his voice—sometimes tremulous, impassioned and dry, nervous—made me think of his tendons stretched taut

Suddenly, without my having asked him anything, he said to me, "I'll tell you why I don't like women anymore."

Smiling, I examined his face, and I knew he was about to make a big confession: it would be sincere and a little naïve.

"Tell me."

"Have you ever noticed that I am sometimes off in a dream?"

"Yes."

"Then I should tell you that I'm always thinking about

the same thing. I can't seem to stop. When I was in Lucca two months ago, I fell in love with my uncle's wife."

"Did she love you?"

"Actually, she loved me before I loved her."

"I'm listening. Speak slowly."

"I had begun a portrait. Her husband asked me to paint it . . . I never want to call him 'uncle' again. He is my uncle all the same. But he wasn't in Lucca much because he's a traveling salesman, and so we had the chance to talk often. You should also know, I was staying in their house.

"I should also say that I knew how she felt about me for over two years.

"But I had left right after that, before any secrets had passed between us. When I went back this time, two months ago, it didn't seem like there was anything to lose anymore.

"I never wanted to love her. I didn't quite believe that she was trying to tell me something whenever we were alone. I was waiting for her to be the first to admit what she felt.

"But once, I had admitted to her that I needed to be loved, I even cried, and I told her that if a woman ever loved me back, I could die for that woman. It seemed true at the time, though I did exaggerate some on purpose. And then the second time I said it, she grew pale and serious, and said, 'So one mustn't ever love you?' and then she wept. I went to my room. We saw each other again that evening, and I didn't say anything. But, as we parted to go to bed, she held my face and kissed me. I could feel that I was giving less than she was. She kissed me and bit my upper lip, and I'll never forget the sensation of that moment. I barely had the strength to kiss her back; then, instead of going to sleep, we went out into the garden. There was a wall around the garden.

"I said to her, 'Do you think you love me the way I want you to?'

"I needed to be sure, so her answer was important.

"She responded, 'Your uncle is a vulgar man, and he has never understood me. I only want to love you . . .'

"That was the first time."

I laughed and looked at the river, which now seemed made out of dirty, green oil.

I felt so close to him, even if he was neither talking to me nor looking at me, but up the river in silence.

"And then?"

He remained silent.

"Tell me everything."

"Again: I wanted to be sure she loved me, and until I was sure, I was the one refusing her. Before going down to her husband at breakfast the next morning, she came to my room and kissed me."

Fossi put his hands over his eyes.

"It's like I can still see her when I begged her to let me see her — all of her."

"What was she like?"

"If only you could have seen her! Then she posed, and I wanted to paint her like that."

I laughed again. But he looked at me so seriously, I stopped laughing.

It was as if Rome were closing in on us: the dykes on the river, the houses, the sky.

He punched my arm hard to distract me. Then he continued: "She wanted to run away with me at all costs; she was prepared to bring all of her jewelry. We planned to escape to a village in the Alps where I had studied. I'm still thinking of going back there."

"Why didn't you go?"

"It was my fault. I wrote an anonymous letter to my uncle telling him everything. I even told him where we would be, so that he could find us together. In fact, that's how he did discover us."

"And so?"

Fossi stayed quiet for a long time. I watched him intently, and he knew he had to go on, although he was less open when he did.

"She denied everything and left. She pretended to be furious with both of us."

"But you did it all wrong! There must have been some other way to end it."

"I wanted my uncle to know everything; I wanted to humiliate him. Because he didn't think I was smart, and he didn't understand my artwork."

"But couldn't you have been more considerate toward the woman who loved you?"

"I wanted revenge, because of how she had trapped me."

"I don't understand you."

So Fossi began. "You can't have any idea how highly I thought of myself back then, and that I thought it was necessary to stay away from all women. I needed my uncle to know that I was worth more than him—in every way. That's why I wanted him to keep me away from her."

"And you've never seen her again?"

"Never again. My uncle believed her, not me. He wrote to me last week, saying he was prepared to forgive me for ever having invented such a thing."

"Don't you think you should at least answer him?"

"Absolutely not! I can't write to him, although my mother has stopped sending me money from America. I'm sure that if I went back, it would be exactly the same as before."

"And how would you act with her?"

"If she even made the slightest mention of it, I might hit

her. Because I don't want to be taken for a liar; and that's the most important thing."

"You're saying you never loved her?"

When I said this, my voice was choked with pleasure. Which pleasure I could only control by thinking about how much I hated him. For if I had met that woman, her love and her mouth would have melted me. I was the one feeling remorse for how she'd been treated — his remorse. My desire was paralyzing.

But my friend felt just the opposite, and I did understand. Besides, it was a matter of pride, he never would have admitted I was right.

He crossed his arms and looked at the steeple of San Pietro; it was barely visible.

Assuming he wanted to feel stronger than me, I asked him, "Would you like to go there together?"

He had no idea of the conflict within me and was almost scornful when he answered, "We're fine here. Actually, let's go sit on the wall."

But I stayed where I was, standing. I lit another cigarette off the one I had just finished. We stood like that for some time without speaking, and it seemed as if our friendship was suddenly over. I looked at him, and every time he met my eyes, he looked back at the river. Finally he said, "Listen, it's starting to rain."

Two soldiers and a man with an open umbrella passed by. It was only drizzling, and one of the trees growing along the Tiber covered us adequately enough. Nevertheless, I felt alone now, and I wished he would leave.

I thought of writing a long passionate letter to that woman.

He took a silk handkerchief from the breast pocket of his jacket and handed it to me, explaining, "This was a present from her."

Immediately, I began to hope that he still loved her. I asked him tenderly, "Do you always carry it with you?"

He started laughing. And I asked him, "So why are you carrying it around?"

"It's just a souvenir, nothing more."

"Are you happy you have it?"

"You can have it if you want. Smell. It's still perfumed — like when she first gave it to me."

I looked in his eyes; I was angry and impatient. I said coarsely, "You keep it."

"Whatever you like."

He put it back in his pocket, and said, "Let's go now. It must be late."

He took my arm again, but there was nothing more to say.

It rained harder, and we walked quickly. The tables of a sidewalk café were wet with rain. The colors of the posters seemed more vivid, and the electric lanterns leaked purple light out over the cobblestones of the street.

When we parted in Piazza Venezia, he said to me, "I might not be going back to the trattoria."

"So when will we see each other again?"

He didn't answer and climbed onto a passing tram. And ever since, I have been in love with that woman.

(1917–20)

THE MIRACLE

. . .

Francesco Appesi was feeling more and more alone. Having wept and suffered for over twenty years granted him the certainty that he lived according to the purest emotions, emotions he'd never had as an adolescent or even as a young man. He'd come to a point in which his work seemed even more like a dream than did his dreams. He was at a point where he didn't need anyone to feed his spirit or his will. And he became frightened in those rare moments when he went back to being his same old self, for he felt weaker. He was at a point where he loved without needing to be loved back.

And then, springtime! And death became almost unacceptable. He opened the window, and the air made his eyes moist. All he could see were the roofs and the top halves of houses—from everywhere, everyone, everything coming together—shocks of new grass peeking out between one house and the next. Enough to know that spring had arrived.

In his room, he looks to the head of his bed, where there hangs a Madonna he had bought one Sunday for a dime on his way into the church of Santa Maria Novella. On the stoop of the door to the cloister, a cemetery without bodies, there was an old man selling amulets from a drawer taken from a nightstand. He will never forget—there was an old woman there, too, selling candles wrapped in bunches and propped up against the door. There: a young woman, blind, her hair wrapped in a stained red rag. That face, without eyes, didn't seem to have a mouth, or ears, either. Her arms flailed about, never resting; her body was soft, flaccid, as if she had no bones.

Francesco has faith in his Madonna.

Today he feels that it is all over—even his friendship with his closest childhood friend. But he doesn't care. He has a wife and two children; he loves his family in the sight of God. And he is convinced that he's no longer the same person he was when he married or in the first few months of father-hood. The distances behind us are by now so great that we don't regret them even if we have taken the wrong road. Rather than turn back, one moves willfully forward into the mistake.

And Appesi's madness doesn't end here; it grows every day, becoming more perfected, more refined. If it first appeared as ordinary insanity, then today, it's become an intellectualized version of illness. But he doesn't recognize this. Ever since he was a child, he's gone on faith and suffered so much—his suffering sanctified by his determination. He's been so good that he deserves anything—even to go crazy.

He's also thought about not eating. When he goes to bed, after saying his prayers, he always regrets that he's not one of those hermits who thinks only of God and subsists on crusts of bread.

Appesi works at the library in Florence. His beard is so white it seems like it's still blond. Baldness has given him a forehead that starts at the crease of his nose and extends back to the middle of his head; his ears are so long, they reach his chin; he's very skinny and has hair on his knuckles. His children are ugly, and it's impossible to figure out how his wife's face ended up in such a state—only her mouth still looks like it once did. All the rest is bloated; her proportions have changed. Her face is always the same color, except for right after a meal—then for two hours it goes vermilion. It's become impossible to determine, through all that flesh, what's passing through Signora Emilia Appesi's mind. Her nose, cheeks, chin are so stacked with meat they no longer belong to the world. Her arms, too; they're short like two stumps. She couldn't possibly use them for anything. How does that explain why she's so tall?

Francesco tells her, "Buy two pots of flowers for the window sill in the living room."

His wife never does what he tells her to, because she forgets.

Or, he tells her, "We'll cook baccalà tonight."

And Signora Emilia ignores him, because when she's out shopping, she only buys what's there in front of her.

If he asks her to fetch him a book, she doesn't do it, because, after all, the children are more nimble than she is. If he asks her to get salt for the table, she doesn't listen, because she doesn't want salt. But Francesco doesn't get mad, because as soon as he looks at her face, he forgets what he had asked for in the first place.

Signora Emilia never has anything to say, but she listens.

And then when he goes to the library, he has the impression that all the books are alive, that all he has to do is think about it and the books will move themselves. The library is enormous. There are rooms of shelves only he knows about. The cards, catalogued by him in his spidery calligraphy, are like live creatures, and so are the names and titles on the spines of the books. He thinks he has conversations with the plaster busts. And if one of those busts should ever be missing one day, he would be inconsolable; he wouldn't be able to comprehend the loss. Everything that he sees through his eyes in the library has its place there, and there it must stay. So, for him, Florence is always the same, the same people, the same churchbells.

At fifty years old, he still dreams that his mother is angry with him, that his brother chases him until he wants to throw up. Those are nighttime dreams that for years and years have come back to him as if he were in the past moment, with the same sensations, the same emotions.

Before installing electricity in his house, he used to break pieces of wax off the candles and play with it, rolling it in his fingers for hours at a time before throwing it away. He doesn't understand music—that is the only thing he's never understood—but he would have liked to have been a musician. This particular desire always comes back to him, especially in the spring.

The day had to come in which Francesco Appesi no longer even recognized himself—though for years and years gone by, he'd been restraining himself from passing judgment on his feelings.

He came home that day from the library and was nearing his house in Via della Scala. The wind was blowing, and his eyes filled with dust. But there! Look up, at the end of the road, there are all those green trees in the sunlight. And he looked up past the houses for the sun and seemed to feel pleasure at the sight of all those open windows, letting in air and light, as if carried on the wind. A handcart, the covered kind, used to carry milk and bread, had been left by the sidewalk. It seemed squashed. He stopped to look at it, the way little boys do, and he had the impression that the whole road was colored with youthfulness and it was squeezing his heart. Because even though, as has been made clear, he liked springtime, the rays of sun made him feel the weight of his years. He was on the verge of becoming upset, and he rushed home, believing that he'd find his wife there and her face might even be happy. He envisioned a face for her that he couldn't quite imagine. And he wondered why he'd never experienced her voice as something so sweet that he'd want to thank God for it. There was sunlight even in the kitchen. His wife was standing at the stove, and in that light, she really did seem different from all the other days. He thought that if he spoke to her, he might start weeping.

In that moment, he was beside himself. He believed that he had another wife and that he was in love with her. He went into the bedroom, and the Madonna had moved by herself to the desk, where she was standing tall, but not rumpling the papers under her. He thought she held a bouquet of flowers in her hands, and he thought he heard her say, "Francesco, you want to stop living. You want to die now. But I will make it so that you are reborn. Then, I promise, you will never suffer again."

Francesco thought he answered, "That would make me so happy. That's exactly what I've always wanted."

"Then you must leave home right away. You must not turn back. Don't speak again, because this is the only way you can realize death. It is a fake death, but it is equal to the real thing."

And then the Madonna added, "Put me back up on the wall."

He went over to her and picked her up. His heart was quivering. He believed he was holding a hammer in his hands and had to put nails into the wall. But the hammer kept striking his fingers, and the pain made him stop.

Then, before he started crying, he asked the Madonna, "Why must I still suffer?"

But sunlight flooded the room, making it impossible for him to hear her answer.

When his wife called him to dinner, he secretly made the sign of the cross, and everything returned to how it was before. But Francesco couldn't explain to himself how the Madonna could have suggested such a thing. His conscience was uneasy, and the next morning, he went to confession. The priest, who knew him well, was astonished and offered him a vague explanation just to keep him from feeling so very afflicted. Francesco ended up believing that he'd fallen asleep from exhaustion and, without realizing it, had dreamed it all.

But a new mania seized him in the library. He needed to learn by heart what was written in every book on the shelves. At any cost, he needed to know. He'd take the ladder, grab a book, and speed through it, reading here and there, whatever struck him. And then, he'd move on to another book, and then another, without ever stopping. He read until he couldn't breathe, and his eyes couldn't take anymore.

Signora Emilia was, of course, exactly the same as before, and she didn't notice anything different. Only, she did ask him why he was always thinking. And he insisted, "I don't think!"

But he was frightened of his Madonna and within a few months experienced the most unexpected miracle possible. He convinced himself he was a child and that his wife was his mother. He had to hide the fact that he was a child so she wouldn't get mad at him. So he'd pretend that he had something to do, and he'd walk out to the country, hands deep in his pockets — the way he used to, during school vacation. If he weren't so worried about getting caught, he would have gone running down the road along the hedges. Instead, he altered his pace so that he walked with even more gravity. That way, he was out of danger. He was the only one who knew with delicious certainty that, deep inside, he was a child. And he could smile at his own childishness. How privileged he felt among men! No one was equal to him!

But he was the kind of child who didn't need wooden soldiers or jumping beans. When the wind blew and made everything move, there was no telling what creatures he thought he saw dancing on the tops of the grain. He would go up to a tree as if it had called to him by name. And he would sit in its shadow, every so often lifting his eyes to the branches, because they made him laugh. He'd dig his fingers into the wormholes in the dirt. He walked along the longest furrows in the fields. He picked up clumps of earth with his hands. He pulled stalks of wheat out of the ground to squash their white flowers. He never tired. He watched the water run. He hugged the trees.

This is how he amused himself, and he was jealous only of his own children.

(1917–19)

THE CLOCKS

...

Bernardo Lotti had a clock for every room in his house, including the bedroom. In the parlor he had four. They were antique clocks, grandfather clocks, and they were almost identical except in size. They had wooden faces decorated with roses, bouquets and garlands that were painted around the numbers. One of the parlor clocks looked like it had been born there, out of the wall, and had just kept growing until it was bigger than all the others. For twenty, maybe thirty years, that clock had never been moved. Its brass knockers looked as if they weighed a hundred pounds. The black hands were sharp, like the blades of a knife—spinning as if they had something to slice, something to kill. The tick-tock was like breath. Its face, once painted white, was now a dirty, unidentifiable color. The sharp hands seemed to mow down the tiny rose bushes with each pass. Termites had gnawed tiny holes like so many pinpricks into the wood. When the hour chimed, it was transfixing, and you could get caught there, listening to that voice, losing count of the strokes. It was a simple, soft song, and you listened in expectation of some message, a word. The rust on the gears seemed sweet and quaint. The other three clocks in the parlor were barely audible, as if muffling their chimes in deference.

The clock in the bedroom had always been the most elegant. It chimed the hours quickly, as if it were worried about interrupting something. The ugliest one stood in the kitchen.

There was one in the hallway too, but you only saw it when the door to the hallway was ajar. It had always hung there on that wall in the dark—because there weren't any windows. When Lotti went to wind it, it always seemed as if it were about to fall down. A guest coming into the hallway would start and turn at the sound of the pendulum's sweep.

Thus there were, in all, seven clocks.

Lotti's grandfather had been a clockmaker and had kept these clocks at home for himself. They survived because Lotti's father had kept them up out of devotion to his father and to keep his memory alive. Bernardo had done the same. Ever since he was a little boy, it was his task to wind the clocks. Now he still did it out of habit.

Lotti had married a beautiful girl from down the road. They had two children, both of whom died before their sixth birthday. His wife died before her fortieth.

His father had left him a delicatessen; but he didn't have much desire to work, so he sold it and lived off the modest proceeds, remained a widower, and didn't really do much of anything.

Every morning he woke early and went to get a coffee at the same place where he'd always gone. He sat at the same table and was served by a waiter he'd known since childhood. The cups were still the same cups, with a double line of red painted around the rim—there wasn't a trace of the gold that had also been there once. The metal spoons had yellowed.

He took the same walk every day in La Lizza, the gardens of Siena, favoring the traffic of the boulevard where all the carriages drove, where the soldiers marched with their companies, where the schoolchildren and the young people chased each other, pulling handfuls of leaves from the hedges as they ran—hedges trimmed with such uniformity that from a distance they looked painted.

He'd walk up to the Fortezza and circle around and around the barracks—so flat and white—and duck into the shadow of each and every rampart, hesitating when he came across two lovers who, just like him, didn't want to be seen.

From up at the Fortezza, he could look out over the city and easily find the two windows of his own room. They were nestled among the roofs that, from this side of San Domenico, looked like they were about to tumble down. The houses themselves stood in an endless queue, each one trying to edge far enough out from the line so that it would be just a bit more visible.

At the end of the walk, he'd buy a newspaper—always the same one. He'd go back home to read, open the windows wide, and sit in their light. His windows looked out over a dark road, where a row of arches connected the houses on one side of the street to those on the other.

When the clock at City Hall struck midday, Lotti went to the Piazza del Campo to eat in a restaurant called Trattoria della Speranza—the one with the green awning and the white letters painted on it. He always ate the same thing. So it was a special occasion whenever he tried a new dish, and he'd have half a liter of wine more than usual. It was his custom to offer a glass of wine to the lemon monger who was always sitting on a stool in the doorway of the trattoria; he rested there, holding his basket, empty by that time of day, upside down over one knee. One hand would be tucked into his pocket, jingling the copper coins he kept there. He had a blade of straw or hay tucked into his mouth, he was red in the face, and there was always some kind of heat blister on his cheek or the tip of his nose. His mustache seemed to grow sparser over time—there were only two or three bristles left. His eyes were clear and wet; his hair was slick with sweat. He'd wear his hat tilted over one ear, even though it was too small. He wore blue shirtsleeves, no jacket, and he'd ripped open his shoes so they wouldn't rub against his corns. He was still a young man, but was already half crazy: two months out of every year, he spent in an asylum. He'd get better without any liquor, and he'd leave. He always said hello to Lotti, as if he were obeying orders. Lotti, as was his manner, barely returned the greeting, even though it pleased him—so much so, in fact, that he'd have been terribly offended and never come back to the trattoria if the lemon monger hadn't said hello.

"It's a beautiful day, Signor Lotti!"

And, looking up at the sky, to the tops of the towers sprouting from the Sienese roofs, Lotti would answer with a smile, "It most certainly is."

Then he would sit down. He always made sure there was a chair at hand so that he could settle himself right in.

His legs trembled a little, and he'd grown thin. He walked with a cane. He wore shirts with collars, but every last one of them was frayed at the cuffs. His clothes were old, but he didn't want to have new ones made. He figured he would die soon and wouldn't have much chance to wear the new clothes, and so it would be a waste of money! He always explained it that way to the lemon monger—who would shake his head and swear up and down that Lotti was going to outlive him.

After lunch, even in the winter, he'd go to sleep. When he woke, before putting his jacket back on, he'd make the rounds of his clocks.

A lit cigar in his mouth, he'd look them over one at a time, spending as long as half an hour on each one. You could find him standing before a clock, watching the hand run half a turn, waiting for it to chime a second time. Then he'd leave that clock and stand in front of another. He stood straight, even if there were plenty of chairs in the room to sit in.

The clocks were hung high, almost from the ceilings, and he had to tilt his head upward to look at them. But while he was looking, he always had a lot to think about, reflecting on his entire life.

Occasionally while looking at a clock, he would remember something for the first time, and that would depress him, because it made him feel old. He'd bow his head and pace from one room to another, not daring to look up at the clocks again. By then, the house belonged more to the clocks than it did to him—even he had that impression. They were the lords, and he was their tenant.

Once, he moved the bedroom clock ever so slightly to one side; the effect of the pure white wall underneath was stunning—it was as clean as when he'd been a newlywed! And the rose bouquets seemed to flush with new color; he could even smell their perfume, the scent just like the flowers his wife had tucked into his buttonhole one of their first mornings together. His bride's mouth was still lovely then, and her hair was black—it didn't matter how much her face had suffered, and that the mole on her chin had grown too large. It didn't matter if her neck became swollen, her skin was still smooth; and when he saw her bare shoulders, he half wanted to kiss them, although after she was dressed, he didn't think of it again.

All of Siena knew about Lotti's clocks. People actually thought he had even more clocks than he did, because they had moved everything out from his grandfather's workshop after he died, and none of it had ever been sold.

Even though he had spent some time working with his

father in the delicatessen, he gave the impression of a man of means. His manner was polite and distinctive, and he never discussed the shop with anyone. When he realized that someone else was thinking of it, he'd blush like a child and cut short the discussion. It wasn't that he was ashamed, but that he was embarrassed about having stopped working before he'd gotten old. In everything else, he felt a kind of sorrow; he felt too alone—more alone than if he'd never had a wife or children. Sometimes this solitude gave way to a real melancholic desperation—but he'd smile about it. He was always pleased, fulfilled, and without regret. As he saw it, he had a responsibility as a young widower to maintain his sanity. He'd wanted his existence to be bound to a woman, so that he could only become a human being at her side, but her death had closed off that door, shutting him into himself. Why had his children died? It made him feel like a being apart, a force that was closer to God than to man.

Looking at a diagram of his family tree, the green and red banners of the family crest, made him feel young again, as if his ancestors were all still alive. The Lotti family had so many ancestors! Once upon a time, a Lotti had been the standard-bearer to the Sienese republic; another had been the lord of a castle in the Maremma. Bernardo felt a swell of pride thinking of it. But now it was all useless! The crest even had a thread of silver in it, and he couldn't bring himself to look at it. What a loss! Standing under the banner, its ends blowing in his face, walking with a slightly haughty step. The standard-bearer was his favorite, and Bernardo felt such an affinity to him, he became convinced that they even looked like each other. No one ever thought about his family anymore; and so he, too, had to stop.

His greatest sadness was that he didn't have a son. The Lotti family would disappear upon his death. It wasn't even clear why he'd been put on this earth. There were other people flourishing now, people he considered enemies simply because they were so different from him. Young people who had different ways of doing things. He never would be able to understand their ways or laugh at the things they thought were funny. His own youth flooded him with irony—a combination of nostalgia and bitterness. And then a random association made him remember his inconsolable passion for his wife, his need to keep loving her. The joy it gave him had made him feel alive and made him feel even more inconsolable because of how different it was from the spirit of his soul. That joy never emerged to stand next to him anymore; he had to content himself with the knowledge that it had been there once. Like his ancestors had been there once, and in his mind they were still there, watching him intently because he wasn't able to have a son. So he didn't have any power to offer them. And yet it seemed that they wanted more than anything to give him the motivation to live more!

But death took Bernardo long before he had the time to fully understand any of this. He died of pneumonia. He received communion for the last time as if he'd just come to church on a Sunday morning. He watched the sky up until his last breath. Until his last breath he listened to his clocks— even the one that stood in the dark passage.

His face stiffened into the expression of a person who turns to look at something he has bumped into in the dark— just about to get up and take a walk, to buy a glass of wine for the lemon monger. He didn't have any relatives, so two women, tenants in the building, washed him, and dressed him hoping they might receive something in compensation— money that he might have hidden in his bureau or tucked in a pocket, even though they knew that he kept his money in an account.

Then, since there was no one to wind them, the clocks stopped one at a time — the one in the bedroom facing the bed seemed like a corpse itself. The last one to stop was the biggest one, the weight on its pendulum dragging down to the floor. But it didn't stop until the next day, after Lotti was in the hallowed ground.

The landlord was anxious to clean the rooms, and he had all the clocks taken out and sent to the dealer in the market where farmers did their Saturday shopping.

That year, the lemon monger never came out of the asylum.

(1919)